One More Genie

by
Doctor MC, Mad Scientist
doctor_m_c@hotmail.com

Ὑπό Τῷ
Ἡλιῷ

HYPO TO HELIO BOOKS
Houston

Paperback ISBN: 978-1-938293-26-9
Ebook ISBN: 978-1-938293-27-6

This is a work of fiction. Names, characters, places, and incidents are the product of the author's imagination, and any resemblance to actual persons, living or dead, business establishments, events, or locales is entirely coincidental.

Those chapters set in Unionville, West Virginia have references to both *1632* by Eric Flint and to the *Hunger Games* trilogy by Suzanne Collins, both authors' works being connected to the Appalachia region of the USA.

All sexually active characters are eighteen or older.

Front-cover render art by: Commotion22

Contact Doctor MC, Mad Scientist at: doctor_m_c AT hotmail DOT com

BISAC Subject Headings:
Fic009010—Fiction > Fantasy > Contemporary
Fic027030—Fiction > Romance > Fantasy
Fic050000—Fiction > Crime

HYPO TO HELIO BOOKS, 2427 Clearbrook Dr., Missouri City, TX, 77489-6061

Prologue
Six Djinn Are Geniefied

June 15, 632 B.C.
Arabian Peninsula

Aleser of the Green Tribe of Djinn loudly claimed, to anyone who would listen to him, that Sumera of the Blue Tribe of Djinn learned her *djinni* magic from demons. And yes, Reader, that is as much of an insult as it sounds like.

Perhaps Aleser was joking; perhaps Aleser truly believed what he was saying. It didn't matter, because the Blue Tribe demanded that Aleser be turned over to them for "correction."

Green Tribe's answer, stripped of all its rude Arabic, was "No way are we handing Aleser over."

Blue Tribe declared war on Green Tribe. Blue Tribe is always certain of everything they do, so Blue Tribe was sure that they would win the war against Green Tribe. But then the Pink Tribe allied with Green Tribe. The Brown Tribe, wisely, stayed out of the whole shebang.

(Brown Tribe *djinn* have brown hair, brown skin, and brown eyes. They could pass for human, without shape-shifting. Which is good, because Brown Tribe *djinn* can't shape-shift. Their *only* magic is to *foom* themselves, plus whatever they're touching, from Point A to Point B.)

Anyway, a place and time were set to start the Djinn War. So everyone in the Green Tribe started practicing their repulsion-spells.

(Which seems odd, at first. Why bother to knock down an enemy *djinni* when you know how to kill him, by freezing him or by immersing him in water?)

Fatima, a loyal Green Tribe *djinni*, asked Ashnadim, Chief of the Green Tribe of Djinn, that same question.

****

June 17, 632 B.C.
Amid sand dunes, somewhere in Arabia

Fatima spoke the words, and made the gestures, that Ashnadim had just taught her.

FOOM. Fatima grinned as a five-cubit-tall, three-cubit-diameter, cylinder of sand and shimmering air was replaced by a like-sized cylinder of water. Which immediately collapsed into the cylindrical tub that now existed in the sand dune.

Ashnadim, Chief of the Green Tribe, smiled at Fatima. "I knew you would be quick to master this spell. Very good."

Fatima's grin turned wolf-like. "I can't wait to give Kharmesh a bath." Kharmesh was the tallest *djinni* in Blue Tribe. Also the strongest, the loudest, and the pushiest.

Ashnadim's smile disappeared. "*Do not* use this spell. Even if we are losing a repulsion-spell battle, do not use it."

"Why not? We could rid the Earth of that pack of loudmouths, so why settle for pushing them away?"

"Listen to me, Fatima. *Don't even think it.* If you water-swap one *djinni* in the Blue Tribe, they might not know who did it—"

"Which leaves me free—"

"*But* they will respond by water-swapping two from the Green Tribe. *At least* two. Then we will respond by disappearing more than two of theirs. More Blue and Green *djinn* will disappear every second. In less than a minute, the Green Tribe will all be gone. Or worse—"

"*Worse?*"

"—the remnant of Green Tribe will have to surrender to Blue Tribe, *and* we Greens will be so few in number that the humans will no longer fear us."

"But if I'm not allowed to use this spell, why learn it?"

"So that if water-swapping starts happening, I want you to kill all the Blue Tribe *djinn* you can before you yourself are 'given a bath.' "

"So you're telling me, plan on repulsing them hard. Even though that won't kill them."

"Yes. The beings of the Blue Tribe aren't really *djinn*, they are wailing human infants. Make them hurt often enough, and Hakeezib"—Chief of the Blue Tribe—"will say *Please stop, please stop, we give up.*"

****

The next morning
June 18, 632 B.C.

Solomon, King of Israel, had just been awakened by a palace servant when they both heard a voice: "SOLOMON, OBEY THE ANGEL OF GOD."

Solomon's sleepy eyes snapped open. Standing in a corner of his bedchamber was a being that could only be an angel: It had white wings, and silver eyes in an inexpressive face.

Solomon replied, "I am here, O Angel. What does God command?"

"PUT A SADDLE AND SADDLEBAGS ON YOUR HORSE. GATHER FOR YOURSELF FOOD AND WATERSKINS FOR A JOURNEY, AND A PURSE FILLED WITH COPPERS. THEN RIDE YOUR HORSE TO THE CITY MARKET."

"What about bodyguards? What about my sword?"

"LEAVE THEM. GOD WILL PROTECT YOU."

The angel disappeared then. Solomon sent his trembling servant off to the stables, to pass on orders to the stablemaster.

A time later, when Solomon's black stallion reached the edge of the city market, the angel appeared again—

—with its wings flapping to hold the angel above the ground. The angel's face was level with Solomon's face, though Solomon was astride the biggest horse in Israel.

"SOLOMON, GO TO THE STALL OF ELKANAH THE BRASS-SMITH. BUY FIVE BRASS OIL LAMPS AND ONE BRASS BOTTLE WITH STOPPER. LOAD THE PURCHASED BRASS INTO THE SADDLEBAGS BY YOURSELF."

The angel disappeared again, and Solomon walked his horse forward.

Elkanah blinked in surprise when Solomon rode up in front of his stall. Perhaps the man's surprise was because there was no herald loudly announcing *Make way for the king!* and no bodyguard shoving shoppers aside.

Solomon had been puzzled by the angel's strange shopping order. But once at the brass-smith's stall, Solomon saw for himself that Elkanah was selling only five oil lamps; Solomon was buying his entire inventory of them.

Solomon had not realized how accustomed he had become to servants, until he had to load the oil lamps and the brass bottle into his saddlebags without help. Those brass containers weren't small, and it took Solomon three tries, with everyone in the marketplace watching him, before he got everything to fit.

Solomon climbed back onto his horse, not knowing what else to do. The angel appeared then, and the crowd gasped.

"What now, O Angel?" Solomon asked.

"GOD HAS A TASK FOR YOU, WISEST OF HUMANS," the angel replied.

That's when horse and king rose into the air, making the crowd gasp again. A semitransparent white bubble formed around Solomon, his horse, and the angel, and the bubble hurried south from the marketplace.

Inside the bubble, it was as quiet as a library, so Solomon heard the angel clearly. The angel did not speak for long, or need to. The rest of the trip was spent in silence, with Solomon thinking hard.

****

One hour, 27 minutes before the Djinn War
The agreed-upon battlefield-to-be

Some *djinn* of the Green Tribe were elsewhere, practicing their spells, but Fatima was on the battle line.

Except it wasn't a true battle line yet. Instead, it was a line of Blue Tribe *djinn* facing east, and a line of Green Tribe and Pink Tribe *djinn* facing west, and the two lines were trash-talking each other. Aleser (Green Tribe) and Thrim (Pink Tribe) were insulting Sumera (Blue Tribe); Kharmesh (Blue Tribe) was insulting Ashnadim (Green Tribe) and Sigvard (Pink Tribe); and Fatima was loudly informing everyone in Blue Tribe that their leader, Hakeezib, was uglier than a human leper and more stupid than a dog.

Only Fatima's close friend Jerngert (Pink Tribe) was keeping quiet. Jerngert looked nervous.

If Fatima was honest, she was nervous, too. Getting hit by a full-blast repulsion-spell *hurt;* and she was going to be hit with lots of battle-grade repulsion-spells before one side or the other surrendered. Then, too, there was that other worry: Would someone in Blue Tribe "give Fatima a bath" before sunset? Would Fatima *die* today?

The number of Green Tribe *djinn* plus the count of Pink Tribe *djinn* was a little more than the count of Blue Tribe *djinn*. But Blue Tribe had a unified command, and the Green Tribe-Pink Tribe alliance definitely did not. Fatima couldn't begin to guess what that would mean, once the battle started.

Then Fatima saw something out of the corner of her eye. She turned her head to look—

Coming rapidly closer, from the north, was a white bubble. The bubble landed on a sand dune, and disappeared.

Now revealed by the vanished bubble were a gold-crowned human man atop a black horse, and an angel.

The human's knees nudged his horse forward, but the beast moved slowly. The human was making himself an easy target for any fireballs thrown his way, which puzzled Fatima. *Is the human so stupid he doesn't realize the danger he's in?*

The angel flapped its wings slowly, to match the snail-like speed of the human and his horse. This also puzzled Fatima. *Why is the angel deferring to the human? Humans don't deserve to be deferred to.*

The human's face and posture were relaxed, and his horse's pace slow, as if he were passing between two lines of human servants, instead of two lines of human-hating *djinn*. When the human had come close to Hakeezib, Chief of the Blue Tribe (to his right), and Ashnadim and Sigvard, Chiefs of the Green and Pink Tribes (to his left), he stopped his horse.

As slowly as if the human were half-asleep, the man got off his horse. *Clearly* he didn't realize the danger he was in, or he would never have done anything so disrespectful.

"I am Solomon, king of Israel," the man said. "God says to stop this war and for you all to leave this place."

Hakeezib laughed. "I care not whether you are king of the whole human world. I don't take orders from *humans*."

"In this, we agree," Sigvard said. "I care not a bit about humans."

Solomon said, "But *God* cares about humans. Your repulsion-spells will take human lives and destroy human villages, and God will not allow that."

Ashnadim said, "But I don't see God here. I see a human who is not even wearing a sword, and *one* angel."

Solomon walked around the horse, and removed three oil lamps from the saddlebags. He set the oil lamps on the sand.

"Your last chance, tribes of *djinn*. Stop this war and leave this place. *Now*."

Hakeezib said, "You bore me, human. *You* leave now, before I hurt you."

"Um," Jerngert said. But when all the *djinn* in all three Tribes turned to look at her, she said no more.

Nobody else said a word.

Solomon looked at the angel. "Who started this fight?"

White lightballs appeared in front of the angel; the lightballs flew to Aleser and Sumera, and floated over their heads.

Solomon said to the angel, "I need a troublemaker from Pink Tribe."

Seconds later, there was a white lightball over Thrim's head.

Solomon said, "You, male of the Green Tribe: Enter this first oil lamp, which becomes the Vessel that Binds you. You, female of the Blue Tribe: Enter this second oil lamp, which becomes the Vessel that Binds you. You, male of the Pink Tribe: Enter this third oil lamp, which becomes the Vessel that Binds you."

The three *djinn* thus commanded—Aleser, Sumera, and Thrim—turned into smoke and entered the three oil lamps. Fatima was close enough to Aleser to see the surprise on his face; he was not doing any of this by choice.

For a moment, there was complete silence.

Then the silence continued, while Ashnadim, Sigvard, and Hakeezib exchanged glances.

Hakeezib said, "Kill the human. The human must not escape."

Ashnadim and Sigvard nodded.

****

The angel had not left Solomon's side. The angel did not speak words, or gesture, but the semitransparent white bubble again formed around the human, his horse, and the three oil lamps.

Blue, green, and pink fireballs blasted the white bubble. Repulsion-spells hit the white bubble and broke up, without the white bubble even wobbling.

Inside the bubble, Solomon smiled at the *djinn*. Calmly he took the reins of his horse and walked the animal away from the attacks—turning his back on his attackers in the process.

As Solomon moved a few cubits away, the wall of the bubble moved with him. In less than a minute, the three oil lamps were on the outside of the bubble.

"Get Aleser's lamp!" Ashnadim yelled.

FOO-F-FOO-FOOM! Suddenly the three lamps were surrounded by *djinn* of all three tribes. Fatima saw Nadaar bend down to pick up an oil lamp, and Fatima expected him to *foom* over to Ashnadim and to hand Aleser's lamp to his tribe's chief. But instead, Nadaar started cursing.

That's when Fatima realized that Nadaar's counterparts in Pink Tribe and Blue Tribe also were angry; while the three oil lamps had not moved one pinky-width.

Nadaar turned his back on the oil lamps to face Ashnadim, and Fatima was surprised to see green smoke below his elbows.

Nadaar said, "No matter what I do, or how hard I try, I can't stop my arms from turning to smoke when I touch Aleser's oil lamp."

Nadaar was getting everyone's attention except Fatima's. Fatima watched Solomon, inside his white bubble, take two more oil lamps and a brass bottle, and lay them on the sand.

"RETURN," the angel said. There were flashes of white light near the first three oil lamps, and Nadaar and the other would-be rescuers reappeared where they'd come from.

The white bubble vanished again.

Now-exposed Solomon seemed unworried. Calmly he said to the three tribes' *djinn*, "I told to you all, God's word for you: Stop this war."

"NO!" everyone yelled.

"You turned your ears away. I took a hostage from each tribe, to humble you. You have not turned from your course, except to try to kill me. Again it will cost you."

****

Solomon picked up the middle oil lamp by its handle, using his right hand. With his left hand, he slapped the metal body of the oil lamp. The oil lamp shook in Solomon's hand, then blue smoke poured out. Within seconds, Sumera stood before Solomon.

He smiled at her. "You have the prettiest blue hair I've ever seen. What is your name, pretty *djinni?*"

"DON'T TELL HIM!" Hakeezib yelled.

Sumera looked ready to strangle. "Go—Go—Master, I am Sumera, of the Blue Tribe."

Hakeezib said, "I told you not to tell him!"

Solomon waved the comment away. Then he looked at Sumera and said, "Correction: You are Sumera, *formerly* of the Blue Tribe, now one of three bound *djinn*. Sumera, how long before the war is scheduled to start?"

"Don't tell him that, either!" Sigvard yelled, just before Hakeezib yelled the same.

But Sumera summoned her scrying ball, worked it, vanished it, then said to Solomon, "There are slightly over sixty-eight minutes left before the war starts, Master."

Sumera turned to look at the gathered *djinn*—Blue, Green, and Pink. "I had to tell him. I couldn't *not* tell him."

Solomon said, "Now Sumera, look at the *djinn* of Green Tribe. Look at their faces. See anyone you hate?"

Sumera said, "I hate *everyone* in Green Tribe, Master."

"Is there one face you see whom you *especially* hate?"

"Nadaar. He acts like Ashnadim's lapdog. Nobody in Blue Tribe would act like that; Blue Tribe has more pride."

"Hear me, O Sumera: Walk up to Nadaar, kiss him on the lips, do him no harm, then walk back here."

Djinn don't walk—they *foom* wherever they want to go. But Sumera turned away from Solomon and began walking. Fatima could clearly hear Sumera's footsteps cross the sand, because nobody spoke a word.

By the time Sumera got to Nadaar, Sumera was so angry that her face was bright blue. But she carried out all of the human's orders.

Solomon had not let go of Sumera's oil lamp. When Sumera again was standing in front of Solomon, he ordered, "Go back in your Vessel, Sumera."

Sumera clenched her hands into fists. But her resistance did her no good; she turned into blue smoke, all of which entered the spout of the oil lamp that Solomon held.

Solomon put Sumera's lamp down, then stood up and faced the three tribes. "These three will be the servant of whoever summons them, and only a human can summon them from their Vessels. Each bound *djinni* will grant their human master three wishes, under certain conditions, and the bound *djinni* will obey any nonmagical command that his or her human master will give."

Then the human *smiled* at the furious *djinn*. "Any comments?" he asked.

****

"You will suffer, human!" Kharmesh yelled. "All the human soldiers in your Israel cannot stop Blue Tribe from coming after you. Your every breath will be agony, from today till your Fated Death! I, Kharmesh, swear this by—"

Solomon silently pointed to Kharmesh, then pointed to one of the empty oil lamps at his feet. Kharmesh turned to blue smoke and entered that oil lamp.

Silence fell among all *djinn.*

Then Fatima yelled, "Why are you doing this to us, Son of Dust? None of us have hurt you!"

Solomon answered, "Yes, Daughter of Smoke, none of you has hurt me. None of you has hurt my human brothers. Not yet. But you will, if this war happens. Thousands of thousands of humans will die because of your repulsion-spells, and human innocents will suffer, and this must be prevented."

"So what?" Fatima said. "I don't care if humans die. Because they're *human.* I don't care whether human innocents suffer. Because they're *human."*

The angel came over and murmured in Solomon's ear. Then Solomon and the angel had a quiet conversation. Fatima could not hear a word.

When the angel moved away, Solomon bent down and picked up the brass bottle. His left hand held the bottle by the neck; his right hand wrapped around the stopper. Then he looked around at all the *djinn* of all three tribes.

Solomon said, "There is one *djinni* here who is an innocent. She does not want to hurt anyone, even her supposed enemies. She deserves not to suffer, whether by her enemies, or God, or me. But I will make her suffer unfairly, so that the rest of you will sympathize with those close to her."

Fatima was getting a very bad feeling about Solomon's words.

Solomon pulled the stopper from the bottle. "I command you to enter this brass bottle, which becomes the Vessel that Binds you . . . Jerngert of the Pink Tribe, friend of Fatima."

"*NO!*" Fatima yelled.

But Fatima could do nothing but watch, as Jerngert pink-smoked and entered the brass bottle.

Solomon stoppered the brass bottle, set it down on the sand, and picked up the fifth oil lamp.

Waving the oil lamp to emphasize his words, Solomon said, "Hear me, O *djinn* of the three tribes. I will take a she-*djinni* from the Green Tribe now, and Bind her into this Vessel. I do this by the power of God, and you cannot stop God. God sends you a warning: If you indeed fight this war, God will no longer Bind you *djinn*, He will kill you. Blue, Green, or Pink, no Tribe may defy God."

Solomon then looked at Fatima. "I need a female *djinni* from the Green Tribe, Fatima. It seems you volunteered."

Chapter 1
I Meet The Rescued
Kids' Parents

Saturday, May 15, 2010, evening
Outside Rhonda's house

"I enjoyed the party, Rhonda," I said. "Thank you for letting me come."

I was leaving Rhonda's costume party. Redhead Rhonda was dressed as Jessica Rabbit; I—Marvin Harper, nicknamed "Shorty" until recently—was dressed as the very tall, very muscular Captain America, complete with shield.

"I'm glad you came, Marvin," Rhonda now said. "You and Tim were a big help with those nasty girls."

Rhonda was referring to Almira and Elvira LeClerc, who had threated to plant drugs in Rhonda's toilet after they'd been caught party-crashing. Instead, thanks to Tim Hanson and me, Almira and Elvira had been arrested.

Rhonda added, "And that other thing you did, with the Witter kids? That was heroic of you. Brave, too."

I shrugged. "I did it because it needed doing."

During the party, our half of the state had lost electricity for twenty-seven minutes, and Rhonda's house did not have a land-line telephone. So when I had discovered that a house on Rhonda's street was on fire, that people had been trapped inside, and that nobody at Rhonda's party could call the Fire Department, I had run across the street.

I had wound up rescuing two small children, Katie and Larry, from that burning house. I had also, without intending to, saved the life of the kids' dog, Blackie.

Rhonda now said, "I feel sorry for Julius and Nancy, when they find out what happened tonight. They're in for a shock."

Then she stepped forward, and looked to her left. "Speaking of whom, it looks like the Witters are home now."

I turned to look where Rhonda was looking. In the driveway of the ruined house, a silver SUV now was parked. In the front yard, a man, who was holding a flashlight, and a woman were talking to Kimberly Paulsen (the sixteen-year-old babysitter). The children, Katie and Larry, were holding hands as they and Blackie listened to the older people talk.

"Rhonda, I need to talk to your neighbors," I said.

I shook Rhonda's hand again—and was still surprised when Rhonda did not turn into my touch-slave. Then I turned and walked toward Katie, Larry, and their parents.

****

It was four-year-old Katie who spotted me, as I was crossing the street diagonally. She started pointing at me, yelling, and jumping up and down. Five-year-old Larry ran up to me (*not* looking both ways as he entered the street), and grabbed my hand.

"Captain America, we told them you rescued us, but Mom didn't believe us!" Larry exclaimed. "Come meet Mom and Dad, and then they'll hafta believe Katie and me!"

By now, there was a flashlight beam in my eyes. "Good god, *look* at him!" I heard a woman's voice exclaim. She sounded amazed.

I could understand her amazement. I was now 6′8″, and I was now richer and more muscular than anyone deserved to be. Eight days ago, I'd been a shorty at 5′2″, the butt of jokes at my high school, a victim of bullying and helpless to stop it, and I was as *un*rich as you could get. So now I was still mentally adjusting to all the new goodies in my life.

Isn't it amazing, Reader, how one old brass lamp, with Fatima the green-eyed genie in it, can change your life?

****

I faced the children's father and stuck out my hand. "My name is Marvin Harper," I said.

You know the drill, Reader. Just by shaking hands, I magically turned Julius Witter, then Nancy Witter, into my touch-slaves. Then I said to them, "Let's just be friends," then both adults became (mostly) free of my enthrallment.

I said to Julius, "I came over to see if there was anything you needed. Anything I could help you with."

Nancy looked at me in confusion. "You already saved our children. What else *is* there?"

Julius laughed bitterly. "Is there anything I need? Yes, ten grand, right now. But ever since that factory closed, this whole city has been in a housing slump, so good luck with us getting a second mortgage. Especially after our house has burned down. So my choices are either, move the five of us—"

I said, "*Five* of you? Are you counting the dog?"

"I'm pregnant," Nancy said. "That's why we went out tonight: to celebrate."

"Oh, jeez," I said.

Julius said, "So my choices are either to move the five of us into whatever house we can buy with the insurance settlement, or. . ." His voice got hesitant.

"Or what?"

"A guy at work has a little gambling problem. He knows somebody who would loan me ten K."

"Oh jeez, you're talking about a *loan shark?* Don't do that!"

Julius shrugged. "My family has to have a place to live, and the OB/GYN doctors have to be paid. What can I do?"

Then Julius looked at the burned house and sighed. "Shit, I could be in debt for the rest of my life, because of this goddamned fire."

I made a snap decision. "I'll *give* you ten grand. Then you won't have to borrow from a loan shark."

Nancy said to me, "You're how old, mid-twenties? How can you get your hands on ten thousand dollars so that you can give it to a total stranger?"

I said, "Mid-twenties? No. I'm eighteen, but—"

Kimberly (the babysitter) asked, "Are you rich, Marvin sir?"

Little Larry said, "Captain America is strong! Of course he's rich too."

I laughed. "Actually, folks, I *am* a little rich. All you need to know is, If I promise you ten thousand, I'm good for it."

What an understatement. I was worth thirty-two *billion*. At age eighteen. How absurd.

Nancy asked, "But *why* are you doing it? People don't just give thousands of dollars to other people they've just met."

I replied, "Because you need the money. Also, because I didn't earn my money. I'm set for life because *one time*, I visited a cranky old man in the hospital. So why keep my money, when I can do good by giving it away?"

****

The next afternoon, the Witters were holed up in a motel room. Lawyer David Dodd knocked on the motel-room door, then he gifted Julius and Nancy Witter with ten thousand dollars in cash from my wall safe.

I would have worked that errand myself, except that I was hosting a pool-party orgy at the time.

Chapter 2
ALLAHU AKBAR On The Airplane

THREE YEARS, NINE MONTHS LATER
Wednesday, February 12, 2014

Last April, I had decided that I wanted to own my own jet and be allowed to fly it around.

Ten months later, I still needed 23.2 hours of solo flying to qualify for my private pilot's license. So when I decided to attend a stockholder's meeting in California, I had to fly in a big commercial jet instead of in my private jet.

Because I'm big and because I'm rich, I always fly First Class in a passenger jet. In this case, that puts me very near the cockpit door. (Not that I thought in those terms, when I took my seat on that flight.)

Boarding at the same time as I did were two Arab-looking men. They sat together in the same First Class row I did, on the other side of the aisle. They never relaxed.

Okay, fine, I occasionally notice one passenger who gets fidgety on an airplane—I figure he has a fear of flying. But *two* such passengers, sitting together?

These two are up to something.

An hour later, the cockpit door opened up, and the captain came out. He was walking toward the forward galley (which was only a few steps away). But then everything turned to shit.

The window-seat Arab guy stood up, and he had a white, ceramic gun in his hand. He fired two shots, and the captain fell down.

As soon as the captain dropped, the Arab guy in the aisle seat pulled a gun out of a little bag, stepped out into the aisle, and ran for the cockpit door (which was still open).

Well, two can play that "element of surprise" game. I jumped out of my seat, ran over to Window-Seat Arab, and punched him in the stomach as hard as I could. He bent over, and I brought my knee up against his chin.

He went down then. I didn't take time to check whether he was dead or unconscious.

By now the First-Class passengers and the First Class flight attendant all were screaming.

I was handing Window-Seat Arab's ceramic pistol to the passenger just behind him when a voice came over the airplane's public-address system:

"Hello, passengers, this is *not* your captain speaking. *Allahu akbar*, God is great. You make ready to die."

At that, the airplane tilted down into a steep dive.

Now *everyone* on the airplane was screaming.

Except me. I ran into the cockpit. (Which was made easier by the fact that it was downhill.)

The copilot was dead on the cockpit floor; I had no choice but to step on his hand.

The hijacker-pilot didn't turn around at first, figuring I was his companion. When he noticed me in his peripheral vision, he grabbed the gun out of his lap and started to aim it at me.

One of my hands grabbed his wrist. The other hand grabbed his gun by the barrel and yanked it out of his hand. I might have broken some of his fingers; I didn't care.

He hissed in pain, then managed a taunting smile. "You not hurt me, American. Who fly the airplane?"

"Me," I replied.

He looked surprised, right up to the moment that I grabbed his head with both hands and snapped his neck.

I stuck his gun down the back waistband of my pants, yanked the hijacker-pilot's corpse out of the pilot's seat, sat down in the pilot's seat myself, and—

—pulled the airplane out of its dive.

Reader, that sounds a lot more impressive than it really was. Mostly, leveling the airplane from a steep dive took strength, which I had plenty of. And yes, the cockpit of a 747 has lots of dials and controls, but some things haven't changed since the Wright brothers flew.

After I stopped the airplane's dive, it was just a matter of contacting air-traffic control and giving them a situation report. ("First the bad news: I'm flying an airplane I'm not legally qualified to fly. . . .")

Achmed had already talked to the tower in Omaha, so I'm sure Omaha was surprised to hear from me. After that, I got on the PA system and told the (other) passengers that it was not Achmed flying the airplane anymore, it was I.

Whoever was minding the store in Omaha was no lazybones; he grabbed a 747-qualified pilot named Chuck, and Chuck talked me through landing the airplane.

An hour later, the airplane was down and we were rolling on the runway. That is when I heard, through the cockpit door, loud applause.

That applause was nothing compared to the cheer that I got when I stopped the airplane on the tarmac and shut down the engines.

Was I a hero? Not at all—because I knew that my Date Of Fated Death was at least six years away. I'm just the guy who managed to get himself in the pilot's seat, then managed to land the airplane in Omaha. With help.

Chapter 3
Parole Hearing . . .

FIVE MONTHS LATER
Monday, July 21, 2014, 4:00 p.m. EDT
Greentree Lake State Women's Prison

Almira and Elvira LeClerc were up for parole on their drug convictions. I had words to say about that topic.

I was in a mellow mood as I walked into the prison's conference room. The main reason I was feeling good was that Victoria Allblue had spent the entire trip "entertaining me" while I'd been driving.

But now, after Victoria had chewed on several breath mints and had fixed her lipstick, she again looked like what she was (officially): one of my attorneys on retainer.

When Victoria and I walked up to the long table in the prison conference room, six people were already there.

On the other side of the table were the two men and two women of the Parole Board.

On our side of the table were Rhonda (the almost-victim of the twins' crime) and Michelle Landrieu-LeClerc (mother of Almira and Elvira). Michelle and Rhonda were glaring at each other.

When we walked in, Michelle went from glaring at Rhonda to glaring at the two of us. "Well, if it isn't the Harem-Pimp himself, Marvin Harper. Not to mention, my *turncoat* attorney, Victoria."

Victoria replied serenely, "I am convinced that there is no conflict of interest between what I did four years ago as your representative, and what I do now as Mr. Harper's representative. If you feel otherwise, you are free to complain to the relevant state bodies. However, they are not bound to keep anything secret."

I smiled at Michelle, the fire-breathing feminist. Right now, I had an approval rating in the high nineties within the state, and an approval rating in the low nineties nationwide. Michelle would have a shitstorm rain on her head if word got out that she had ever told her attorney to file a frivolous lawsuit against the mega-popular Marvin Harper.

Now Michelle scowled and turned around, as a man on the other side of the table pounded a gavel.

Bang-bang-bang. Gavel Man said, "This parole hearing, which is in regards to Almira Sharon LeClerc and Elvira Karen LeClerc, will now begin. Bring in the prisoners."

Both twins were wearing orange jumpsuits, and had their hands handcuffed in front. Almira gave me a bedroom smile—but then, Almira *always* gave me a bedroom smile. Elvira, on the other hand, looked nervous.

After some pompous boilerplate, the Parole Board let the women speak for themselves.

Almira said, "I've already learned my lesson. I can't tell you how awful it is to know that Marvin Harper is disappointed in me. If you let me out, I promise I won't do anything to disappoint Marvin Harper ever again."

Elvira said, "I have to be with my sister, Almira. Nobody is more important to me than my sister. If Almira doesn't want to break the law, then I won't break the law either, and you can take that to the bank."

Bang. Gavel Man rapped his gavel once. "Thus ends the prisoners' statements. Ms. Allblue, as the prisoners' legal representative during their trial, do you have anything to say to us?"

Victoria stood up. "My clients have a close bond. I feel it is in their best interest that you parole them at the same time. Even if that means that you deny both twins' parole now."

As Victoria sat down, the twins didn't say anything, but Almira elbowed Elvira in the ribs. Almira also shot Elvira a look that I was sure meant *If we don't get parole, it's your fault, twin.*

Bang. Gavel Man rapped his gavel again. "Now we will hear from anyone opposed to giving parole to the prisoners, then hear from those in favor of their parole."

Gavel Man asked formally, "Is anyone opposed to giving parole to these women?" Gavel Man was looking straight at Rhonda, the red-haired stripper.

Rhonda stood up. "These two women crashed a costume party I was hosting. When I told them to leave, they threatened to plant drugs in my toilet and then call the sheriff to arrest me."

"So says a woman who takes her clothes off for men, for money," Michelle said. "Whereas my daughters were students at Gorshin University, till you *lied in court* about them."

Rhonda said, "Yeah? One of your little darlings, I forget who, had drugs in her purse. You're either lying to the Parole Board, or you don't know your daughters well."

Rhonda turned to face the Parole Board again. "Those two showed no remorse on the day they were arrested. I have *no* doubt that if you let these two walk, sooner or later somebody will get on their bad side, and *she'll* be wearing the jumpsuit on a bogus drug bust, like *I* almost did."

When Rhonda sat down, Gavel Man asked, "Does anyone else wish to speak against granting parole to the prisoners?"

Silence.

Bang. Gavel Man said, "Now we will hear from anyone in favor of early parole." He was looking straight at Michelle.

Michelle stood up. "I'm sure that is merely a one-time lapse of judgment. I raised my daughters to be strong—"

"By which she means *Man-hating bitches,*" Victoria murmured to me.

"—not to commit crimes," Michelle continued. "Well, except for killing an abusive husband. I'll say it again: I don't expect my girls ever to do anything like this in the future. *If* they even did it at all."

Michelle sat down.

Gavel Man looked at me. "Am I correct, Marvin Harper, that since you have not spoken out against the prisoners' parole, that you are in favor of it? Even though you were present at the party at which they were arrested, and you were called as a prosecution witness?"

I stood. "Am I in favor of their parole? It's complicated. I am convinced that Almira has reformed. As for Elvira—"

I glanced at Elvira, whose face was white with fear. Elvira knew that I had every reason to trash-talk her.

"—I am convinced that Elvira means it when she says that if her sister Almira behaves, then she will behave too."

I glanced at Elvira again, after I sat down. She was looking at me in amazement.

Back in 2010, I had given strict instructions that Paula Sarin was not to be allowed in my house (because I knew she wanted to steal Fatima's lamp, but I didn't mention that part). Elvira then not only had let Paula Sarin enter my house, but Elvira had extorted fifteen hundred dollars in cash from Paula. So yes, Reader, you would expect me to say bad things about Elvira.

Now the skinny brunette on the Parole Board looked at the other members and said, "We should take seriously what Marvin Harper says. He's the 'hero billionaire,' after all, and already his Harper Foundation has helped many people."

The other woman on the parole board jumped in: "Plus he's spent time with the prisoners, both in monthly prison visits and . . . during their time out on bail."

Michelle said, "Let's not get carried away. I'm glad he's arguing for my daughters today, but while they were out on bail four years ago, he had them serving as French maids in his mansion. He was exploiting them!"

Almira said, "Mother, it wasn't exploitive. I'm glad I French-maided for him, and I'll gladly do it again." Almira gave me another bedroom look.

I smiled at Almira, then I looked at the Parole Board. "That brings up another topic: How will these two earn money after prison? I offer them each a job at the Harper Foundation if she wants it."

"Oh, I want it, I want it!" Almira said. "*Anything* to spend more time around you, Marvin sir."

"If Almie works there, then I'll work there too," Elvira said. But she didn't act happy about it.

"And where will they live, while they're working at the Harper Foundation, huh?" Michelle demanded of me.

I said innocently, "They can always move back in with me, if they choose to."

"But you're *married*," Michelle said. "To that bimbo big-breasted former cheerleader."

"She has a name," I said. "Anna Kay Henderson Harper."

"Anna Kay is *so* understanding," said the skinny brunette on the Parole Board. "She thinks it's great that every woman in the country wants to fuck her husband."

When Michelle glared at her, the brunette said, "Hey, I'm telling the truth. Anna Kay Harper gets interviewed on TV *a lot*. And she always says the same stuff."

The skinny brunette, meanwhile was giving me a look that said *I don't care if you're married, I want to fuck you too.*

The skinny brunette's reaction did not surprise me. When Fatima had granted six wishes of mine all at once, she had become both creative and generous in her wish-grants. Since that day, if I would touch someone (and if they did not already have a strong negative feeling about me), they instantly became my touch-slave. If I then said, "Let's just be friends," that cancelled *most* of the person's enthrallment, but they still treated me favorably. Similarly, if I would sit near to someone for a long time, my magic pheromones enthralled them.

Clearly, that is what had happened here. Without my intending to, I'd affected the two women on the Parole Board. Now they would gladly get naked if I told them to; so they voting for the twins' parole was only to be expected.

So I smiled at Almira and Elvira. *Don't worry, you'll be out soon.*

Though part of me wondered whether I was acting foolishly. Each twin was evil, which explained how the twins wound up in prison. Complicating things, Elvira was magically enthralled to Almira, Almira was enthralled to me, but Elvira was immune to all *djinn*-based mind control (including mine). Was I doing the wise thing, trying to put Elvira back on the street?

Chapter 4
. . . And The Drive Home

Victoria smirked when I started the Lincoln Town Car. "I can't believe you're a billionaire, and yet you're driving a five-year-old car."

I said, "Why trade it in? It runs great, so buying a new car seems silly. *Plus* I got this car for free, from Uncle Warren. *Plus* it has headroom." Which at 6'8", I desperately needed.

Victoria glanced around. We were now away from the women's prison, and zooming through the countryside. She said, "Mm, speaking of *head*, shall I go back to what I was doing during the drive down?"

I smiled. "If you don't mind."

"I don't mind one bit. In f—*zzz*."

Victoria fell back against the passenger seat and started sleeping—in mid-sentence. A moment later—

FOOM.

—there was a flash of green light from the backseat.

"What's up, Fatima?" I asked, surprised.

****

The voice of my genie was angry: "A tall, balding, redhead guy put a bomb in your car while you were inside the prison."

"*FUCK!* Was it set to blow up when I started the car?"

"No, it's set to go off when he remotely activates it. But he hasn't tried that yet, so I can't do anything to him."

"Ah, because he hasn't committed himself in human terms to an attack on me."

"Exactly, Mast—"

There was a green flash from the backseat.

Fatima said, "Boom, you're dead—or would be. And whoever this guy is, now I own his life."

"Anything I need to do, Fatima?"

"Please pull over and stop the car. If he's watching us, let's make it easy for him."

I slowed down and moved onto the shoulder. There was another green flash.

Fatima said, "This guy knows he didn't get you the first—"

Still another green flash from the backseat. By now my car was stopped on the shoulder.

I said, "Gotta give the guy points for persistence."

"I'll sure give him *something*," Fatima said. "Something he won't like."

There were two more green flashes, one second apart.

Fatima said, "I'm bored with this guy." She gestured—

FOOM.

—and a tall, balding, redhead guy appeared in my backseat.

"WHAT THE FUCK?" he exclaimed.

He was wearing a cross-draw, underarm holster. He went for his gun, even as Fatima went for his forehead.

Fatima had Hyperspeed. The redhead man didn't.

For the next minute, he trembled and shook as Fatima memory-read him.

When Fatima broke the connection, she said to me, "Meet Michael `Red Mikey' Smith, contract killer. He was in Delta Force, but he got kicked out of the Army for striking an officer. The Carlino Family hired him after you and I broke up that loan-shark cartel."

I said, "Yeah, the loan sharks *would* be pissed at me, wouldn't they?"

Meanwhile, Smith had been dazed, but now clearly he'd come out of it. He quick-drew his pistol and took turns aiming his pistol at Fatima and me. "I don't know how I got inside your car, Harper, but I'm hired to kill you, and that's what I'm going to do. You too, Green Eyes."

I was calm at that moment. Mainly because I knew that my Date Of Fated Death was not for at least six more years.

So calmly I said, "You're not the least bit curious why your bomb didn't go off? Or how you got in my car?"

Smith said, "Doesn't matter. You're the fucking Hero Billionaire, so who knows what kind of tricks you can pull with your dough?"

I rolled my eyes. "You're stupid, Michael Smith. You plan to shoot us in this car, which is registered to Marvin Harper the Hero Billionaire? Our murders will be discovered within the hour by the Highway Patrol. Then the police will bring in every crime-scene investigator between here and Poland to track you down."

Smith sneered, "Then I'll have to make sure that your corpses aren't discovered for a while. You two, out of the car."

Somehow Smith had completely failed to notice the sleeping Victoria Allblue. I didn't correct his mistake.

Once Fatima, Smith, and I were out of the Lincoln, I said, "Now what?"

Smith said, "See that gas station?" Near us was a boarded-up, weathered roadside gas station. "March. Behind the building."

Fatima and I marched, with Smith behind us. Fatima started humming a tune from Disney's *Aladdin*.

"You trying to cheer yourself up, Green Eyes?" Smith said.

"I'm already cheerful," Fatima said. "And in a minute, I'll explain why."

"In a minute, you'll both be dead."

One minute later, we were behind the long-closed gas station. Where the three of us were walking, no cars could see us from the road.

"That's far enough, you two," Smith said.

Fatima casually tossed a hand over her shoulder. *Foom.*

"*What the fuck? Where'd my piece go?*" Smith said.

Both Fatima and I turned around. Smith was staring dumbfounded at his curled-fingers right hand.

Fatima said, "I sent your gun to Mount Kilauea in Hawaii, which has lots of hot lava in it. The good news is, that's not where you're going."

Smith stared at Fatima in confusion, saying nothing.

Fatima said, "You ever heard the term *crush depth*?"

Fatima gestured—

FOOM.

—and where Smith had been, there was a seven-foot-tall, four-foot-diameter column of water. Which immediately fell to the ground.

On the ground was a strange-looking fish. Which, as I watched, got bigger and bigger, and then it exploded.

The water on the ground, I noticed, smelled like sea water.

"What did you do with him?" I asked Fatima.

She shrugged. "Bottom of the Indian Ocean."

Then Fatima gave me a feral grin. "I've been wanting to use that particular spell for twenty-six hundred years."

The whole incident seemed like no big deal. After all, I knew at the time that I was in no danger.

But Reader, I made a mistake then. Fatima said a couple of things to which I should have paid more attention.

Chapter 5
Sex With Anna Kay

When I got back to the mansion, I told Anna Kay all about my adventures at the parole hearing. I didn't mention the magically defused bomb.

This had begun to bother me, that I was keeping a huge secret from my wife. Part of me felt I should sit her down and should tell her, "Honey, about Fatima, my housekeeper? She's actually a genie, I'm her master, and everything that makes me special, came from Fatima. And Fatima's lesbian sex slave, the pretend-fembot SJ-1? SJ-1 is actually Sheila Johansson, the disappeared assistant to disappeared Senator Paula Sarin; and by the way, Paula Sarin also is a genie master."

On the other hand, my conscience didn't bother me *enough* yet to make me tell Anna Kay the truth.

Anyway, after I'd told the tale of my words at the parole hearing, Anna Kay said, "That's one of the things I so love about you: You're so *good*."

"Good at what?"

"You're *good* good. I know you don't like Elvira for some reason—"

"I don't, but I'm sorry, honey, I can't tell—"

"But today you went down to the prison, and used some of your time, and charm, and good reputation, to get Elvira out of prison earlier. I am so lucky to be married to you. You're good, you're nice."

I said, "I'm lucky to be married to you too. *You* are good, *you* are nice, and"—I hefted her big, tear-shaped tits—"you're lots of fun to be with."

Anna Kay gave me a smoky look. "You know I want to suck your dick whenever you play with my boobs."

I replied, "I'm feeling like more than that. How about we go to the master bedroom and I fuck you till you see stars?"

"I'm sure that isn't on the Sex Schedule."

Not counting my wife Anna Kay, my genie housekeeper Fatima, and Fatima's lesbian sex slave SJ-1, there were thirty-two women living in my house, and all thirty-two were in my harem. I was getting fucked and sucked by thirty-four women, so a computer-generated Sex Schedule was a necessity for me.

Now I picked Anna Kay up and started walking toward the stairs. "Not by the Schedule. I'm about to have passionate, unscheduled sex—not with my housekeeper, or a *haremée*, but with my wife."

In my arms, Anna Kay gasped and shuddered.

Somehow, in the process of granting six wishes at once, Fatima had set things so that whenever I give Anna Kay any special treatment, she has an orgasm. Anna Kay doesn't mind.

Meanwhile, I was climbing the stairs, with Anna Kay in my arms. When we reached the top of the stairs, we saw Colleen, who was dusting the furniture in the upstairs lounge. Colleen put down her duster and gave me two thumbs up.

Colleen said to us, "I wish you were carrying *me* so easily. Strong Marvin gets me *hot.*"

Anna Kay shook with another orgasm.

A minute later, I set her down in the bedroom. She said in a Southern accent, "You carried me up the staircase, and now you are going to ravage little old me. Fiddle-dee-dee, I love a husband who's *dominant.*"

I laughed. "I love you, Anna Kay." I began to undress my wife.

For whatever reason, she had sworn off anything stretchy since she married me, except for exercise wear. So at the moment she was wearing a light-blue button-up blouse, a purple skirt, and purple shoes with two-inch heels.

I enjoyed unbuttoning her blouse and casting it aside. What was revealed underneath were two glorious mammaries, encased in a light-blue lacy bra. I took a moment to fondle Anna Kay's tits through her bra.

"Mmm, I'll give you till midnight to stop that," she said.

I unhooked the bra, cast it aside, then bent at the waist to take a revealed nipple in my mouth.

Have I mentioned, Reader, that Anna Kay's large and tear-shaped tits are *perfect?*

"Mmm," Anna Kay said again.

But for all Anna Kay's clear enjoyment of my attentions, she was not trying to kiss me, caress me, undress me, or undress herself; she was acting totally passive.

This excited me; my dick started to get hard.

I pulled off her shoes, then I unzipped her skirt; and again, Anna Kay just let everything happen to her.

By now, the only thing that Anna Kay was wearing was lavender-colored, soaked panties. I didn't pull her panties off then; instead, I reached inside her panties and lightly stroked her clit.

"Take me, command me, use me," Anna Kay said. "Take me, command me, use me."

Every time Anna Kay says that, she means it. And every time she says that, with me knowing that she means it, her words get me hard. I was rock-hard now.

"Get me undressed like you're undressed," I commanded Anna Kay. "Everything but underwear."

"I obey, my husband," she replied.

Anna Kay pulled my shirt out of my pants, unbuttoned my shirt, and cast it aside.

But instead of starting on the next article of clothing, Anna Kay's hands began caressing every inch of my chest, back, and arms. "You're so muscular," she kept saying, "you're so strong."

Anna Kay got rid of my shoes and socks by me lifting a foot and she pulling that foot's clothing off of it, just as I had done with her. But before Anna Kay removed my shoes, she had knelt down to untie the laces.

"Is there anything else you wish me to do while I'm kneeling?" Anna Kay had asked.

"Not now," I had replied, but my dick had twitched with arousal.

Now she ran her hands over my still-pants'd legs. "Mmm, you're so muscular, you're so *strong*." Still kneeling in front of me, Anna Kay unfastened my belt and unzipped my pants.

My pants dropped to the floor. I stepped out of them.

Anna Kay said, "Are you *sure* there's *nothing* you want me to do, so long as I'm on my knees?"

I growled, "Right here, right now, *I* decide when I get my dick sucked. You got that, wife?"

"I obey, my husband."

Anna Kay stood up now, and walked up to me, so that her flat stomach was pressed against my hard dick. She reached around me and started caressing and squeezing my ass muscles. "Mmm, so muscular, so *strong*," she said again.

I said, "It's time for sex. Take off your panties."

She did, with a shimmy. When Anna Kay was naked, she said, "Take me, command me, use me."

By now I was myself naked, erect, and hard enough to punch holes in armored plate.

I restrained myself. "I'm going to taste you now," I said, moving down to the end of the bed, "while you're all wet."

"But don't you want to—?"

"I'm doing what I want."

Anna Kay shaves all but a one-inch wide "landing strip" of pubic hair, so getting hairs in my teeth is not a worry.

Licking a pussy when Anna Kay is aroused is very different than when she's not aroused (at first). When she's aroused, her pussy lips are bigger; my tongue can feel the difference. Of course, when Anna Kay is aroused, her pussy smells different.

Does it surprise you, Reader, that I would do such a servile thing as licking my wife's pussy? First of all, I *love* Anna Kay; I've loved her since middle school. Anna Kay is just *nice*. Second, one of the ways that Anna Kay is nice is that she'll suck my cock at the slightest excuse; I'd be a total rat bastard if I didn't reciprocate at least once in a while. Third, licking Anna Kay's pussy is the *only* time, and the *only* way, that I am not obviously the dominant one in our marriage.

By now, after four years of our having sex, I know how to get Anna Kay off. I slid a long, thick finger in and out of her pussy all the time I was licking her clit, stroking her pussy walls in the process—and this sent Anna Kay into several hip-thrusting, hair-grabbing, screaming orgasms.

But all good things must end. I slid up the bed, wiped my face on the bedsheet, and—

"I love you, Anna Kay."

—I kissed my wife.

After I broke the kiss, Anna Kay said, "Something big and thick and warm is poking my thigh."

"It wants to fuck your pussy. Give it a kiss to let it know this is okay with you."

So just as I'd slid down the bed a few minutes earlier for the purpose of oral sex, so Anna Kay moved now.

"Use me for your pleasure, my husband," she said. Then she put her mouth on my cock.

Reader, Anna Kay not only loves sucking cock, she's good at it. She can put her mouth on my absolutely unaroused, flaccid dick, and only seven minutes later, she'll have me spurting. But that was not what I wanted right now.

I let her put her lips and tongue (but *not* her teeth) on me for only one minute. Then I said, "*Stop*. You are delightful, Anna Kay, but now I want to come inside your pussy."

"As you wish, my husband," she replied, lying down on the bed.

She was wet. Slick-wet, slurpy-wet. Her sugar-walls squeezed and caressed every inch of my cock when I first thrust it in.

After that first thrilling thrust, whenever I thrust down, she thrust up, and gasped, and squeezed my back. Her ankles soon locked around my ass.

She took her hands off my back, and used them to grab my head. She pulled my head down to her face and kissed me *hard*. Then she kept kissing me.

"Oh Marvin, *kiss*, my darling, my husband, *kiss-kiss*, that feels so good, *kiss*, you fuck me so good, *kiss*, I *need* it, don't stop, *kiss-kiss*, that's so *good*."

Her skin was hot and sweaty. Soon *my* skin was hot and sweaty. Sweat pooled where our stomachs came together.

Despite all my self-control (from working algebra problems in my head), soon I came hard. As I was seeing fireworks in my brain, I thrust my dick in Anna Kay's pussy as deep as it would go. Then I thought about playing catch with my son.

"I love you, Anna Kay," I said, when I could speak normally.

She replied, "I love you too, my husband."

****

From the way that Anna Kay talks during sex, you would think, Reader, that she's the most mind-controlled woman I know. But the truth is the opposite—

Fatima granted six wishes in four-and-a-half minutes, and she achieved this by combining wish-grants. One wish-grant gave me the magic pheromones and the magic touch that have given me my harem, but which have no effect on Anna Kay. Another wish-grant made me become Anna Kay's perfect man.

Anna Kay's perfect man is the alpha-est of alpha males.

Since I'm so alpha, this frees Anna Kay to play at being the complete submissive. She isn't really, of course—she'd never have made it onto the cheerleading squad.

But Anna Kay acts completely submissive to me when we're private, and I never abuse her trust. So when feminists ask her why she married a man who openly has sex with other women, Anna Kay confounds the feminists with her reply:

"I married Marvin because with him, I get to live out my fantasies."

Chapter 6
Vinnie's Lucky Night

HALF A DAY LATER
Tuesday, July 22, 2:03 a.m. EDT
Several states over from Marvin Harper

Twenty-six-year-old Vinnie Lavagetto was a hit man, but he wanted more out of life.

Right now, his big claim to fame was that he was the great-great-grandson of a cousin of "Cookie" Lavagetto, the Brooklyn Dodgers baseball player.

Which was worth less than a plate of spaghetti, so far as the Family was concerned.

Other members of the local Family were asleep right now. Or maybe getting a blowjob from their honeys. But what was Vinnie doing, at fucking 2 a.m.?

Vinnie was in Podunkville, Massachusetts, sneaking around some lowlife's backyard with a stepladder. Hoping that the guy didn't have a barking dog. Hoping that the guy's neighbors didn't have a barking dog. Hoping that none of the guy's neighbors had insomnia and were right this minute calling the cops on Vinnie.

Sometimes Vinnie wondered if he should have stayed in high school. Maybe he'd be sleeping now, instead of trying to whack somebody at fucking 2 a.m.

Vinnie made it into the backyard without Fido or Spot or Killer announcing his trespassing to the world. So far, so good. He laid the stepladder on the grass and—very quietly, which meant very slowly—extended the stepladder to its full length. The attic of this house was on the third floor, and that was how Vinnie planned to enter the house—through the attic's window.

The climb up the stepladder was *not* fun. For most of the way, the ladder shook with every step. Plus Vinnie was clearly visible to any neighbors who might be awake.

When Vinnie got up alongside the attic window, he was surprised to notice that the glass had bubbles in it. *Whaddaya expect? Old house, old glass.*

Vinnie grinned. This window had glass in it that was hundreds of years old, and Vinnie would get to bust it out. That didn't make up for the blowjob that Vinnie wasn't getting right then, but fun is where you find it.

Vinnie took a deep breath. There was no quiet way to break glass, and the noise might wake up somebody inside the house. But there was no other quick and easy way inside this house, either.

Fuck it. Let's do it.

Vinnie busted the glass, pulled leather gloves over his latex gloves, and climbed through the window.

Vinnie thought, *If I was a big shot in the Family, I wouldn't need to worry about cutting my fucking hand with no fucking glass at fucking 2 a.m.*

The first thing that Vinnie heard, once all of him was in the attic, was—

"George, I'm sure I heard glass breaking."

"Okay, okay, Susan, I'll check it out."

One floor below the attic, Vinnie heard a man's footsteps move along a hallway, then go down stairs. Once the footsteps left the stairs, Vinnie couldn't hear any more.

Vinnie grinned. George could check his first-floor doors and windows all he wanted; the fact that everything was okay didn't mean squat.

But meanwhile, Vinnie didn't move. He wasn't about to give Susan any ideas to tell George to check the attic.

Ten minutes later, Vinnie heard George's footsteps on the stairs, this time moving slowly. George's footsteps moved along the hallway to his bedroom, this time more slowly. Vinnie heard—

"You dreamed the glass. Windows are fine, doors are fine. I'm going back to sleep."

"I didn't dream it, I heard it."

"Good *night*, Susan."

Well, shit. Now Vinnie was stuck in the attic till they fell asleep. Figure half an hour, at the least.

Ten minutes later, he was bored. He clicked his flashlight on, and looked around the dark attic.

The light beam picked up wires that ran from a light switch by the attic door, to a light-bulb fixture overhead. Interestingly, the wires weren't covered with plastic, they were covered with cloth.

Next, the flashlight showed Vinnie a dress on a dressmaker's dummy. Vinnie didn't know anything about women's dresses (except how to take them off), but this dress was fancy enough, and old enough, to go into a museum. That is, if it weren't so bug-holed.

Vinnie saw a rectangular thing that was hidden by a sheet, which had to be a painting of someone in a fancy frame. Vinnie felt no curiosity to reveal the painting.

Whoa, what is this?

The wall of the attic consisted of boards that were nailed horizontally. But one board was free of all but one of its nails, and so it went from the wall diagonally down to the floor. *In* the wall, behind where the board was supposed to go, the flashlight beam showed Vinnie something of yellow metal.

Vinnie wasn't especially curious. He figured that whatever he was seeing was something that a museum might want, but Vinnie couldn't pawn. And in any case, Vinnie was stuck in this spot on the attic floor for—Vinnie glanced at his watch—another eighteen minutes, at the least.

****

Twenty-eight minutes later, Vinnie stood up, intending to walk out the attic door, walk down the attic steps, and make the hit that he'd been sent to make.

But before doing that, he detoured to the attic wall and the yellow-metal thing that was in the wall.

His mild curiosity went instantly to keen excitement when his flashlight showed him what the yellow-metal thing actually was. Vinnie grabbed the brass thing by its handle and pulled it out of the wall.

"You're *shitting* me," Vinnie muttered.

In his left hand, Vinnie was holding a genie lamp.

Chapter 7
Vinnie Does His Job

Vinnie quietly shut the attic door, and quietly descended the attic stairs. He held a silencer-equipped pistol in his right hand, and the genie lamp in his left hand.

Vinnie was wary and alert, but the house seemed quiet.

Descending the attic stairs put him at the end of a second-floor hallway. Vinnie already knew, from hearing them talk, that George and Susan slept in the room at the far end of the hallway, but there were three other doors that Vinnie had to check first.

Vinnie didn't know if the lowlife had any kids. Vinnie hoped not; he really didn't want to kill any kids tonight.

Killing a kid was impractical. You kill a lowlife, and the cops figure "He deserved it," and they only go through the motions at catching his killer. But when you kill the lowlife's wife, the cops up their game. And if you kill a kid, the cops will hunt you to the ends of the Earth, even if the kid's papa was Adolph fucking Hitler.

The first door that Vinnie checked, looked into a tiny room. Nobody was sleeping in here, and the room looked like it was used for storing junk.

The second room had two filing cabinets, computer stuff, and lots of cutesy decorations. Vinnie figured this belonged to Susan. Nobody was sleeping in this room.

The third room had a folding card table that was covered with a plastic shower curtain. On the shower curtain were bricks of white powder, wrapped in clear plastic. Nobody was in this room either.

****

George didn't wake up when Vinnie walked into the bedroom. But Susan did. She took a breath to scream or yell.

Before Susan could make a peep—

Thyoo.

—Vinnie shot her dead.

Then Vinnie woke up George.

Vinnie spoke Tony's message to George. Then Vinnie put the silencer-end of the barrel into George's hair, just above the ear, and Vinnie pulled the trigger.

Two minutes later, Vinnie was out the front door and walking up the street to the van that Tony had loaned him. In his gloveless left hand, Vinnie was holding the genie lamp.

Chapter 8
Vinnie. Kharmesh.
Fatima.

At 11:02 a.m., Vinnie picked up the genie lamp from his bedroom dresser, took a deep breath, and rubbed the lamp.

****

By the time that Vinnie had driven back to Boston, had swapped out Tony's van for his own car, and had driven back to his own house, it had been nearly four o'clock in the morning. Vinnie had been sleepy enough to nearly fall asleep while driving.

Vinnie was renting a house, which came with its own garage-door opener, so no neighbor had seen Vinnie carry the genie lamp from his car.

Tony had told Vinnie that he didn't have to come in today till noon. So normally Vinnie would set the alarm for 10:30 and would have fallen fast asleep.

But normally, Vinnie didn't have a genie lamp atop his dresser.

Vinnie's sleep had been fitful, and it had ended too soon.

****

The alarm clock had awakened Vinnie up at ten. One hour for shit-shower-and-shave, and breakfast, and Vinnie was . . . half an hour from when he needed to leave the house.

Vinnie had given himself thirty minutes, when he was more-or-less well rested, to make his three wishes.

Vinnie wasn't smart, and he sure wasn't educated. But he'd seen a lot of TV shows where somebody got a genie, the guy acted stupid, and the genie played the guy for a chump. Vinnie was determined to not be that guy.

Vinnie rubbed the lamp. The brass lamp shook in his hand like a frantic rat were trapped in it, then blue smoke poured out of the spout. Lots and lots of blue smoke.

The guy who came out of the lamp could've been a pro wrestler—he was that tall, and that muscular. Sure, he wore blue silk pants, and he was wearing blue silk shoes where the toes curled up at the big toe, but the muscles kept the guy from looking froo-froo.

But the guy was definitely a genie. He was wearing a fancy blue turban that was held together by a big blue jewel, he was wearing a blue sash around his waist, and was wearing a buttonless, sleeveless blue jacket. All that blue clothing he was wearing matched his blue eyes.

Not to mention, the genie's blue clothing matched the genie's blue skin and dark-blue mustache and trimmed beard.

"Greetings, O Master of ye Lamp," the genie's deep voice boomed out. "I am Kharmesh, ye greatest of ye bound *djinn*, here to grant to you three wishes."

****

Tuesday, July 22, 11:02 a.m. EDT
Several states over from Massachusetts
In the mansion of Marvin Harper

Virgilia O'Keefe parked her car in the mansion's big garage. Seconds after that, she was in the mansion and fluffing her hair in the foyer mirror. Seconds after that, she was walking, *click-clack*, into the monster kitchen.

Virgilia was now president of the Harper Foundation, so she was wearing a woman's serious pin-stripe business suit. Of course, considering that Virgilia had a wish-enhanced figure, that serious business suit, when *she* wore it, looked like the porno-movie version of such.

When Virgilia walked in, there were about a dozen women in the monster kitchen. Half the women there were cooking lunch, and the other half were eating it.

Fatima, who was supervising the cooking, smiled when Virgilia walked in. "Good morning. Work going well?"

"It is indeed, thanks for asking." Virgilia sat down at her favorite spot at the second table.

Virgilia heard Fatima say to a young woman who was chopping carrots, "Cindy, stop that and start cooking Virgilia's hamburger. Cook it medium, no pink. . ."

Fatima had stopped speaking mid-sentence. Virgilia turned to look at Fatima, and saw that Marvin's genie looked like she'd just been goosed in the ass.

Fatima rushed over to Virgilia, grabbed Virgilia by the wrist, and *dragged* her out of the monster kitchen and into the deep-sink room.

Washing pots and pans at the deep sink was Connie, one of Marvin's touch-slaves. When Marvin had met her, she was a cocktail waitress and a dropout from Ewert Grant High School. But thanks to Marvin's "influence," Connie had returned to Ewert Grant, had earned her diploma, and was now attending classes at the community college.

Supposedly. Virgilia now asked Connie, "Aren't you supposed to be in class?"

Connie said, "I was, this morning, while you—"

Fatima said, "Connie, I need to talk to Virgilia *alone.*"

Connie gave the two other women a sexy smile. "Gee, Fatima, I thought you didn't do girls. Well, except with SJ-1."

Fatima said, "Shows what *you* know. But not right now. *Out.*"

As soon as Connie was gone and the door was shut, Fatima started making gestures. Fatima's scrying ball appeared with a *pop*, floating in front of her face. The scrying ball looked like a fortuneteller's crystal ball that was the size of a volleyball, and Virgilia no longer startled whenever it suddenly appeared.

Fatima made more gestures, and a blue-skinned man appeared in her scrying ball. Once Virgilia got past the shock of blue skin and blue facial hair, she noticed the guy's arrogant attitude. Perhaps the man's rippling muscles had something to do with that attitude.

Fatima made one last set of gestures, and the scrying ball *pop*ped gone.

Virgilia said, "You look unhappy."

"You bet your ration, Jackson, I'm unhappy," Fatima replied. "There's now another bound *djinni* out of Vessel. But is it Sumera, Thrim, or Aleser? Any one of them, I could cope with, though Sumera is Blue Tribe, so she's a bitch. But nope, the bound *djinni* who's out is"—Fatima launched into a long string of Arabic-sounding profanity—"*Kharmesh*. The biggest asshole jerk of three tribes' worth of *djinn*."

"So what are you going to do?" Virgilia asked.

"I need permission from Master to watch Kharmesh. Kharmesh won't care if he causes problems for humans."

Virgilia said, "Marvin's in the computer room, as of—"

Virgilia didn't get a chance to finish her sentence. Fatima yanked open the door and ran off.

****

11:02 a.m. EDT
Vinnie Lavagetto's bedroom

"Greetings, O Master of ye Lamp," the pro-wrestler blue genie said. "I am Kharmesh, ye greatest of ye bound *djinn*, here to grant to you three wishes."

"You talk funny," Vinnie said. "Plus you sorta got a British accent."

The genie frowned. "Indeed I have a British accent, for I speak as did my last master, a loyal subject of King George II."

"If he was a Brit, what was he doing in Massachusetts?"

"What was he doing in His Majesty's royal colony of Massachusetts? Are you softheaded, Master? He was being born there. Living there. Dying there in 1760, many years after I was sent back into my lamp."

"Never mind that," replied Vinnie. "So all that stuff in the 'Aladdin and the Magic Lamp' story, it's all true?"

"Aladdin? I know not that name."

"You're shitting me. C'mon, he's trapped in a cave, he has a magic ring *and* the magic lamp, he marries the princess, Bad-Something—"

"Badroulbadour," Kharmesh said,

"—yeah, her. *And* Aladdin gets a big, fancy palace, even bigger and fancier than the one that Bad-Something's papa has, and *he's* a king or something."

"You pronounce the name strangely," Kharmesh said. "I knew him as Ala ad-Din."

"You *knew* him? You knew Aladdin?"

"Of course I knew Ala ad-Din. He was a former master of mine."

"*Whoa*," said Vinnie.

FOOM. Vinnie saw a flash of green light out of the corner of his eye. When he turned to look, he saw a woman standing in his bedroom.

****

Kharmesh, if Vinnie ignored all his blueness, looked like an Arab. The woman looked Arab too, except she had the colors right—black hair and brown skin. But her eyes were very un-Arab: they *glowed* green, like a traffic light.

Her clothing was un-Arab too. She wasn't wearing a veil or a scarf on her head. Instead, she was wearing green shoes, tight green-denim jeans, and a tight green t-shirt that said "Not Just Another Pretty Face." Inside that t-shirt, the woman had *amazing* tits.

"Behold what ye cat dragged in," Kharmesh said, glaring at the woman.

Then Kharmesh said more stuff to her, in a foreign language. His words sounded insulting. The woman replied back to him in the same foreign language; her tone sounded just as insulting.

"Dammit, Kharmesh, stick to English!" Vinnie said. Then he demanded of the woman, "Who the fuck are *you?*"

"I am Fatima of the Green Tribe of Djinn," she replied with a smile, "hoping I'm not too late for the show. I came here to watch *him*"—she nodded at Kharmesh—"have to grant you three wishes."

"You may leave anytime, Fatima," Kharmesh said. "None did invite you here."

"Yeah," Vinnie said. "*I* decide what woman comes in my bedroom, and when. Leave now, or I'll *make* you leave." Vinnie walked toward the dresser, atop which lay his pistol.

She said, "I apologize for intruding, but I'll be here only till you've made your three wishes. Then I'll leave and you'll never see me again."

"Bitch, I told you to leave *now*." Vinnie grabbed the pistol, flicked the safety off with his thumb, and pointed it at Fatima. "This baby has a great silencer on it. I can pump you full of lead and my neighbors will never hear. Take a hike."

Fatima looked at him, and her friendly face hardened into contempt. Then she said sarcastically, "Oh dear, I'm about to be shot."

She gestured, and a tunnel formed in her chest. Vinnie could shove his hand and arm all the way to his shoulder, and not touch any of her body.

Tunneled-Fatima said, "You can aim every shot perfectly, and empty out your entire magazine, and I'll still be standing. Then the *real* fun will begin, human."

Vinnie didn't like that. "What does the bitch mean, Kharmesh?"

Kharmesh said, "Normally a bound *djinni* like Fatima or myself may not kill a human. But a bound *djinni* may defend herself against an attack against her master or himself. If you try to kill her, even if you fail completely, she may kill you."

Then Kharmesh grinned at Fatima. "But when you try to kill him, you will be trying to kill my master, and I must needs defend him. Sorry, Fatima, ye rules are ye rules."

"You two are *both* stupid," Fatima said with a scornful laugh, as her chest became solid again.

She looked at Vinnie and said, "After you shoot me, I'll magically blind you, and Kharmesh can't do shit because by our rules, I haven't harmed you. Then you'll have to use up a wish to get your sight back."

"Whaddaya mean, that's not harming me?" Vinnie said. "I'd be goddamned blind—that sure sounds like harm to me!"

Kharmesh replied, "She would not rend your flesh, or break your bones, or spill your blood, so the rules say she would not harm you."

"That's fucked up," Vinnie said. "She could abracadabra me, and I wind up having to use a wish to fix it, and you can't just straighten the bitch out?"

Fatima said, "I'm getting bored. I came here to watch Kharmesh have to grant you wishes, and that hasn't happened. As for that squirt gun of yours, human, would you either put it away or shoot me so I can have some fun?"

Vinnie glanced at the clock and said, "Fuck, I have to get going soon." He flicked the safety on, and lay the pistol back on his dresser.

He glared at Fatima. "You win for now, bitch."

Then Vinnie turned to Kharmesh and asked, "You got rules about what I can wish for?"

Fatima said, "James Bond here is smarter than he looks."

Kharmesh said to Vinnie, "All three wishes must be made the same day.

"You may not wish for a throne, nor may you wish to cloud men's minds to grant you a throne, nor may you wish to cloud men's minds so that they will fight war for you. If you wish one of these three forbidden wishes, you forfeit that wish and all remaining wishes. You may not wish that anyone die, or be made so sick or so injured that death comes soon. If you wish one of these three forbidden wishes, you forfeit that wish and all remaining wishes. You may not wish for immortality, your own or anyone else's. If you make a wish like this, you forfeit that wish and all remaining wishes. You may not wish to delay your own or anyone else's fated death by more than 120 lunar cycles—"

Vinnie said, "Huh? How long is that?"

Fatima answered instead of Kharmesh: "It's nine solar years, eight months, and some days."

Vinnie nodded at Kharmesh, who continued, "If you wish to delay your own or someone else's fated death by more than 120 lunar cycles, you forfeit that wish. These are all the rules but one, which I may not tell you until after you have spoken all three wishes."

Vinnie slapped his left fist into his right palm. "I gotcha. I'm ready to wish now."

Chapter 9
Vinnie Wishes

Vinnie said, "I wish for lots of paper money, a million dollars at least, and none of it can be traced to me."

Kharmesh gestured, there was a blue flash, and a soccer ball appeared in front of his face—a soccer ball made of clear glass. Kharmesh gestured again, and images appeared and disappeared inside the big floating glass ball.

"What the fuck are you doing?" Vinnie demanded.

"I am researching how exactly to grant your wish," Kharmesh replied.

Fatima said, "I know how I'd grant it if you were *my* master."

"Yeah? How would you grant it?"

Fatima gave Vinnie a fuck-off-and-die smile. "Since you're *not* my master, I don't have to tell you jack shit."

Kharmesh gestured, then the glass ball floated up above his head. Kharmesh gestured again, there was a blue flash, and paper rectangles appeared on Vinnie's bed.

Every one of which was orange, and which had *500* and *Monopoly* printed on it.

Vinnie yelled, "This is Monopoly money!"

Kharmesh laughed. "One wish made, one wish granted."

Fatima said, "I was thinking of a million in Jamaica dollars, but it's the same idea."

"Not so," Kharmesh said. "A million Jamaica dollars would be worth *something*. This is worth *nothing*. I am more clever than you, Fatima."

Fatima shrugged. "It's the first smart idea you've ever had."

Vinnie said, "Would you two *shut up?*"

Then Vinnie glared at Kharmesh. "You cheated me! This isn't what I wanted, and you know it."

Kharmesh smirked at him. "It is what you wished for. What you wanted does not matter."

Vinnie said, "So that's how you intend to play the game, huh?" Then he got quiet.

A few minutes later, Vinnie said, "I wish that if I say to a woman, 'You are mine,' she will love me and do whatever I tell her, for as long as she lives."

Fatima said, "Except that he can't tell her to make him a king, Kharmesh. You have to add that part."

Vinnie said, "What are you talking about, bitch? I just want to get fucked, I don't want to be no fucking *king*."

"I'truth, Fatima," Kharmesh agreed, "there be no need for your addendum."

Fatima said, "Shows what *you* know, Kharmesh. This country has different laws than in 1742. To keep Solomon's rules, you must put in that restriction."

"Say you," Kharmesh said. He gestured, and his big glass ball floated down in front of his face again.

Vinnie didn't understand the genie needing to research anything. There was no wiggle room at all in the wording of his wish, and Fatima's lawyering was ridiculous.

A minute later, Kharmesh looked at Vinnie. "She is correct. I must needs restrict your wish-grant so that the wenches you bed cannot make you become president."

As Vinnie shrugged, Kharmesh asked Fatima, "Does your master have the like restriction, that he cannot order his women to make him president?"

"Yes," Fatima replied. "But since he has no wish to become president, he never will discover that restriction."

Two or three minutes later, Kharmesh's glass ball floated up above his head. Kharmesh gestured, and a blue-lightning ball formed between his hands. Kharmesh made a shoving motion, and the blue-lightning ball flew through the air and hit Vinnie in the chest.

Kharmesh said, "One wish made, one wish granted."

Fatima asked Kharmesh, "Did you give him what he wanted, except for the can't-make-him-president part?"

Kharmesh smirked at Vinnie. "Mostly."

Vinnie frowned, then said, "Okay, smartass, for my third wish, I wish for a dozen more wishes."

"How original," Fatima said sarcastically. "How clever."

Kharmesh said, "I cannot grant such a wish, Master. Please wish again."

Vinnie said, "Whaddaya mean, you can't grant that wish? You're a genie, you can grant *any* wish!"

Fatima said, "How like a human. Only God can do *anything*, and a *djinni* is not God. So don't wish for world peace either, because Kharmesh can't do that."

Kharmesh added, "God decreed that we bound *djinn* would grant three wishes, and I cannot grant a wish for more wishes because I cannot change the mind of God."

"So there's no fucking way I can get more wishes?"

Before Kharmesh answered, Fatima did: "Weren't you listening? You can't wish for even one more wish."

"Does that answer your question, Master?" Kharmesh asked.

"Yeah," Vinnie said, annoyed.

Vinnie looked at the clock. He had fifteen minutes before he had to get in his car.

Vinnie had one wish left to make, and he had to make it count. How could he make himself a Big Shot in fifteen minutes, when the genie would twist whatever he said?

Vinnie said, "Tell me the rules again, Blue Boy."

Kharmesh's look was murderous, but he did as he was told and repeated the wishing-rules.

Which didn't help Vinnie one bit. How could he rise up in the Family if he couldn't make himself immortal, and he couldn't wish anyone dead?

Vinnie wasn't usually smart. But inspiration hit at that moment, and he saw *exactly* what to wish for, to become the biggest of Big Shots.

Vinnie stood straight. "For my third wish, I wish—"

Vinnie took a deep breath.

"—for a magical power. I can look into someone's eyes, and if within ten seconds I say 'Be blind,' that person will become instantly, completely, and permanently blind. But since this is magical blindness, nothin' will show up if a doctor cuts the guy open."

Then Vinnie looked at Fatima and grinned. "Thanks for the idea, toots."

Fatima looked confused. She had to be wondering, *Why did he wish for that?* Soon she'd find out, if she watched the news. Vinnie had plans.

Vinnie barely noticed when Kharmesh granted his third wish, because afterward, the two genies were arguing again—

Fatima said to Kharmesh, "Don't forget, you have to tell the human about the Last Rule. You're such a slacker."

Kharmesh glared. "I was only moments to ye Last Rule without need of your aid, Green Tribe doxie."

Then Kharmesh told Vinnie the Last Rule: If Vinnie had made an unselfish wish, he could've made three more wishes.

"Sure, pal," Vinnie said, "That's a great-sounding rule you got. Too bad nobody is goody-two-shoes enough to ever get that payoff."

Fatima looked at the ceiling.

****

Tuesday, July 22, 11:17 a.m. EDT
Marvin Harper's mansion, the computer room

FOOM. Fatima had returned. SJ-1 and I each looked up from our computer project.

SJ-1 was leggy and busty, with a beautiful face and sexy lips. She would be absolutely sexy if she weren't bald.

And if she didn't dress and act like a Sorayama fembot.

But all of that was her choice, just as SJ-1 being Fatima's lesbian sex slave was her own choice. Since Sheila Johansson had been offered a guaranteed-granted magical request and this is what she'd asked for, who was I to object? Fatima assured me that pretend-fembot SJ-1 was overjoyed with her life—though none of that joy ever showed on her face.

Anyway, I asked just-returned Fatima, "Did Kharmesh's master wish for anything interesting?"

"Oh, definitely," Fatima said, and recapped the last few minutes. We both were puzzled why Lavagetto had wished to cause blindness, and what he intended to do with such a strange power.

After we discussed that topic, Fatima said, "Master, are you free for the next hour?"

I shrugged. "I'm doing nothing that can't wait. What's on your mind?"

Fatima said, "I want to take you upstairs, and SJ-1 and I melt your socks."

"Sounds good," I replied.

SJ-1 was Fatima's sex slave, so SJ-1's permission wasn't asked. But Fatima made a point of seeking out Anna Kay. The first thing that Fatima said, when we walked into the Electronics Playroom, was "SJ-1 and I are going to fuck your husband. That okay?"

Anna Kay was watching a soap opera on the big-screen TV. She glanced back in our direction, said "Have fun," and turned her attention back to her show.

As we were walking away from the Electronics Playroom, Anna Kay yelled, "MAKE SURE SOMEBODY SWALLOWS HIS CUM."

Two minutes later, Fatima and I were undressing. (SJ-1 didn't undress; SJ-1 never took off her fembot costume except when Fatima ordered her to.)

As soon as my cock was exposed to light and air, Fatima ordered SJ-1, "Suck him off and swallow his semen. Anna Kay will be upset if nobody blows him."

While SJ-1 was deepthroating me, I asked Fatima, "Any particular reason for the unscheduled sucky-fucky?"

She said, "Just those few minutes I spent with Vinnie Lavagetto reminded me why I used to look down on humans. I appreciate *you* all the more now, Master."

Chapter 10
Summit Conference

Tuesday, July 22, 7:30 p.m. local time
A coffee shop in Istanbul, Turkey

Sigvard, Chief of the Pink Tribe of Djinn, entered the coffee shop and looked around.

He saw some human men frowning at him. Sigvard was wearing a rose-pink pinstripe suit, a pale-pink shirt, and a Barbie-pink tie with matching handkerchief. His hair was blond, with a trimmed blond beard. To the human men, all this pink meant *homosexual.*

Besides Sigvard's blond hair, only his eyes seemed to be anything other than pink; his eyes seemed green. Actually, Sigvard's eyes were the same bright pink as his tie, but Sigvard couldn't pass for human with pink eyes. So Sigvard had done a minor shape-shift—voilà, green eyes.

Sigvard had entered the coffee shop looking for two other *djinn,* and raised voices told him where they were—

"She had no right to watch him abase himself, like he were a performing bear!"

"Are you telling me that if he had been free in May 2010, he wouldn't have done the same thing to her?"

Sigvard took a seat in the booth that already was occupied by two "humans." Sigvard gave minimal greeting: "Ashnadim, Hakeezib, good evening."

Hakeezib and Ashnadim appeared to both have brown skin and black hair, which fit with their Arabic features. Hakeezib was wearing a blue suit, blue shirt, and blue tie, to match his blue eyes; Ashnadim was wearing sneakers, shorts, a polo shirt, and a cap, all of which were green like

Ashnadim's eyes. Hakeezib and Ashnadim would seem, to any humans who looked at them, to be brothers.

In fact, Hakeezib was the immortal enemy of Ashnadim, just as Hakeezib was the immortal enemy of Sigvard. But since it had not been an option for twenty-six centuries for the three *djinn* tribes to settle their differences by war, problems got solved by a meeting of the three *djinn*-Tribe chiefs.

"Have I missed something?" Sigvard now asked Ashnadim.

Ashnadim said, "Kharmesh the loudmouth, you remember him? His lamp got rubbed an hour and a half ago, and Fatima *foom*ed over to watch him grant wishes to a human." Ashnadim jerked a thumb over at Hakeezib. "Somebody thinks this is disrespectful to Kharmesh."

Sigvard said sarcastically, "It is indeed disrespectful, because *djinn* of the Blue Tribe are *special*."

Hakeezib said, "We *are* special. If we'd ever had that war, your two tribes would have begged you to surrender."

Sigvard said, "Nonsense. You of the Blue Tribe would have fought until you saw you were losing, then things would have turned nasty. Blue Tribe has no honor."

Ashnadim and Sigvard glared at Hakeezib, who glared back; this was an old, old, *old* argument.

To lift the tension, Sigvard changed the subject: "So what did the human wish for?"

Hakeezib said, "Money, which Kharmesh made sure was worthless. Attractiveness to human women. The ability to cause blindness."

Sigvard said, "*Blindness?* Why would the human want *that?*"

Hakeezib shrugged. "Who knows how humans think? Nobody in Blue Tribe has a guess why he wished for that."

Ashnadim said, "Neither does Fatima."

Chapter 11
Adventures in Pittsburgh

Wednesday, July 23, 2014
At a house on Sunrise Court, Pittsburgh, PA

Anna Kay, Virgilia, myself, and Silas Jones (from Keystone Financial Services) walked up the driveway and onto the front porch. I asked, "Mr. Jones, are you ready?"

"Yes, Mr. Harper," he replied (though I was two decades younger than he). He added, "But I've never done anything like this before."

Virgilia said, "You're going to enjoy yourself, Silas. I guarantee it."

Anna Kay added, "Helping out people always feels good."

I didn't reply; instead, I rang the doorbell with the hand that wasn't holding a briefcase.

A girl about eight years old answered the door. I smiled at her and said, "Hello, is your mom or dad here? We have business to discuss."

Seconds later, a man in his thirties was opening the storm door, and looking at the four of us in puzzlement. He asked, "Can I help you?"

I said, "Mister Peter Norman?"

He nodded.

"I'm Marvin Harper—"

His eyes went wide; he recognized my name.

I continued, "This is my wife, Anna Kay, wearing the royal blue; and wearing black is Virgilia O'Keefe, brand-new president of the Harper Foundation—"

Peter Norman said to Virgilia, "President of the Harper Foundation? Wow, you must handle a lot of money."

I replied, "She does, because I trust her." After what happened in 2010, I trusted Virgilia *completely*.

I finished my introductions: "And finally, this is Silas Jones with Keystone Financial Services."

Peter Norman's face and posture showed instant panic. "Look, I'm sorry we're so far behind. If you give me a week, I can pay you four hundred. I know this isn't even a month's payment, but *please* don't take our house."

Quietly I said, "Please invite us in, Mr. Norman. I want to help you with your foreclosure problem."

Peter and Linda Norman had a son who looked about ten, and the aforementioned eight-year-old daughter. The children were hurriedly sent to their rooms.

We four visitors were given seats on the Normans' living-room couch, which had crayon-marked cushions. The gray living-room carpet, I noticed, needed both to be shampooed and to be replaced.

Linda Norman, clearly nervous, offered us coffee. We all declined the offer. Seconds later, she was sitting facing us, in a red-leather wingback chair that mismatched everything else in the living room. Peter Norman stood next to her chair.

Both husband and wife were looking at us with their faces showing dread.

I said to the Normans, "You're six-thousand-plus dollars behind on your mortgage payments. Keystone has initiated foreclosure proceedings."

They nodded glumly.

"I'm a billionaire. I can easily pay off that amount, and stop your foreclosure."

Linda Norman said, "But you've decided to grab up our house instead. Well, you're not getting much."

I shook my head. "Not so. I asked Keystone what it would cost to clear up the mortgage completely, figuring in both the payments currently in arrears and the payments yet to be made. You've got another nineteen years on your house note."

Peter Norman opened his mouth, undoubtedly to ask me how I knew all this, but he shut his mouth again.

Which was a relief. I didn't want to explain about SJ-1 and her expertise at hacking. SJ-1's hacking skills were as magically augmented as her boobs.

Now I opened up my briefcase. "The figure that Mr. Jones here gave me, the amount that is necessary to pay off your mortgage, is $117,842.56."

I took a thick, business-sized envelope from my briefcase, and handed it to Peter Norman. "That amount is what is in the envelope. In cash and coins. Please count it."

Husband handed the envelope to wife, who opened it. Linda Norman gasped when, sure enough, cash and coins fell onto her lap. At the very top of the bills-stack was a thousand-dollar bill with Grover Cleveland's portrait facing upward.

The Normans counted the money twice. By the time they finished, Peter Norman was blinking often, and Linda Norman had twin tear-tracks on her cheeks.

I opened my briefcase again, and handed Peter Norman a tape dispenser. "Please put the money back in the envelope, tape the envelope shut, and hand the envelope to Mr. Jones."

While they were doing that, I opened up my briefcase, and removed three pieces of paper. "This first paper says that Keystone releases all claims against your property, and declares your title to be clear. Both of you will sign each of two copies, Mr. Jones will sign for Keystone, and Anna Kay, Virgilia, and I will sign as witnesses. The other piece of paper says that the $117,842.56 is a gift from me to you; otherwise the IRS would tax it."

Five minutes later, we were at the Normans' front door. Peter Norman shook my hand (and shook it, and shook it).

Linda Norman hugged me with all her might. Even Silas Jones looked like he was trying not to cry.

Jones gave the Normans a reminder about property taxes (they could still lose their house if they did not pay the property-tax bill). Then we left.

Once we all were back in the rental SUV, Jones said, "I'm wiped out. That was *intense*."

I replied, "Yeah, and we have four more houses to hit tonight. But later tonight, you'll go to bed grinning."

****

Late in the evening, we drove Silas Jones back to the Keystone Financial Services building (since by then, he had roughly a half-million dollars in cash in his briefcase).

We watched Jones till he was safely inside the building. Then I said to Anna Kay and Virgilia, "I feel like taking a walk around downtown Pittsburgh, see what they've got here."

Virgilia replied, "The same thing they've got in anywhere else's downtown: bright lights and dark hearts."

Anna Kay asked, "You're planning on saving some hookers tonight, aren't you?"

"If any hookers need saving," I replied.

****

One nice thing about being a foot taller than the average man: It was easy for Anna Kay and Virgilia (who were still in the rental SUV) to keep track of me when I was walking around downtown Pittsburgh.

I foiled a pickpocket. The good news for him was: I didn't call the cops on him, and I didn't beat him up. The bad news for him was: While I had one of his hands restrained, I emptied out his pockets (his wallet, his house keys, his car keys) except for coins. Whatever I removed from his pockets, I threw down the sewer. Onlookers applauded.

Passersby recognized me—"Hey Marvin, I'm glad you're here, now I feel safe"—and hookers recognized me. Eleven times a hooker sashayed up to me, her moves and smile and eyes promising sex, only to whisper when she got close, "Thanks for rescuing those girls in Miami." Or Denver. Or Lincoln, Nebraska.

Eleven times I asked the hooker if she herself needed rescuing. Ten times I was told "No."

But one time I was told, "Not me, no. But there's a guy three blocks down who's *bad* to his girls." Emily the hooker gestured to her right.

I thanked Emily, handed her twenty dollars, and started walking in the direction she'd pointed. Next, I called Virgilia (who was the passenger in the rental SUV) and told her what the new plan was.

****

Reader, it's been four years since I started rescuing hookers (and four years since I first got myself in the news for that). Pimps react to me differently now. A few will act unbothered if I take one of their girls, even making a dismissive hand gesture as if to say *She isn't important to me. I can always get more.* Many pimps will glare at me, but won't fight me—they know the likely outcome of that.

But then there are those pain-in-the-ass few pimps who make my life challenging.

The few pimps that think that because they have a knife or a gun, and I never carry such, they can win.

As soon as I got near the pimp standing near the entrance to "Mike's Playroom," I knew that he was bad news. All of his women were gathered close around him, none of his women walked over to talk to me, they all were looking at me nervously, and he was glaring at me.

A long time ago, I talked to a professional hostage-negotiator, and what he told me was, "Earn the guy's trust. But never, not for one second, let the hostage-taker feel in charge. Instead, act like *you* are in charge. Treat his demands as requests, which you will trade for, but you never grant outright. You never beg, you never plead, and you never lose your temper."

Now the young man was still glaring at me, and I decided that I wasn't ever going to earn his trust. So, remembering the rest of the hostage-negotiator's advice, I took my smartphone out of my pocket and I called Virgilia.

Twenty seconds later, the rental SUV was stopped at the curb, ten feet away from me, with the SUV's hazard-lights flashing. When Anna Kay and Virgilia could clearly see the pimp, and he could clearly see the rental SUV, I walked over to Mr. Pimp and his group.

I called out cheerfully, "Hello, ladies, I'm Marvin Harper. How are you doing?"

I hadn't ended my phone call; the smartphone was still transmitting. Just to make that clear, I was holding the smartphone down in front of me, like a just-revealed ace of hearts, instead of putting the phone in my pocket.

When I got close, Mr. Pimp said, "I don't want you talking to my girls."

I replied, "I don't care what you want. How are you ladies doing?"

He ordered, "Shut off your phone."

"Nuh-uh. Ladies, is he always like this?"

The blonde who was standing next to Mr. Pimp answered, "Most of the time."

Mr. Pimp back-slapped the blonde's arm, then told me, "I *said*, shut off your fucking phone."

"Answer's still no," I calmly told him.

I brought the phone to my lips and said, "Hispanic male, twenties, has snake-eyes dice tattooed on his neck."

As I was bringing my smartphone down to waist level, Virgilia's voice could be heard speaking loudly and clearly: "Hispanic male, twenties, has snake-eyes dice tattooed on his neck. Got it."

I looked at Mr. Pimp's women and ignored him completely. "That SUV has room for three more people. If you want to go home out of town, I can arrange that."

Mr. Pimp reached behind his back and pulled out a pistol. The whores gasped. Mr. Pimp pointed his gun at me and said, "All my bitches are staying *here*, got me? But you, you're leaving now."

From my smartphone, Anna Kay yelled, "YOU THINK SO? YOU DON'T KNOW MY HUSBAND!"

I said to Mr. Pimp, "That has to be the stupidest thing you've done all day."

A different blonde, who looked to be only seventeen, said, "No, he acts stupid *all* the time."

Mr. Pimp swung around to his right, to aim his gun at the underage hooker. "I should—"

His forearm that was holding the revolver, I gave it a well-aimed, powerful martial-arts kick. This knocked the gun out of his hand, and knocked him off-balance.

Mr. Pimp started to scream; I'd broken at least one of the bones in his forearm.

I was recovering my two-legged stance even as the pistol hit a green-painted door behind Mr. Pimp. Fortunately, the gun did not fire.

The gun dropped to the ground. Again luck was with us, and the pistol did not fire.

I shot my leg out again, this time doing a leg-sweep to put Mr. Pimp on his back. His injured forearm must have hit the ground as he fell, because he screamed again.

I put my size-fourteen right foot on his chest, so he couldn't stand up.

He said, "I'm going to—sss, motherfuck!—get you for that, dickhead."

I said, "I don't think so."

Then I said to the underage blonde, "Would you hand me his gun, please?"

As soon as she did, I dumped all the bullets out, then I put the gun in my pocket. Mr. Pimp called me nasty names.

Before I let Mr. Pimp get off the ground, I searched him for weapons. But after that, instead of holding him till cops showed up, I let him walk away.

****

Nobody got arrested, nobody got killed, and only Mr. Pimp got hurt, so I considered it to be a good night.

Six of Mr. Pimp's women (Annie, Josefina, Latesha, Maria, Sally, and underage Steffi Jo) asked to leave with me. To do that, I had to flag down a taxi for three of the women, and the six women got taken to an open-all-night Wal-Mart in two vehicles. Once I'd bought the six women all new clothes, our rental SUV and a different taxi took the six former hookers to the Greyhound station. Of course I bought all six women bus tickets (for as far away as Vallejo, California), besides giving them forty dollars in cash apiece.

Then Anna Kay drove us back to our motel, where SJ-1 was waiting for us. By this time, it was long after midnight.

And Mr. Pimp's now-bulletless pistol? I threw it in the Allegheny River.

Chapter 12
That Bastard Kharmesh!

Wednesday, July 23, 2014

Even hit men need to eat. After eyeballing the vast white emptiness inside his refrigerator, Vinnie got back in his car and drove to the supermarket.

Two girls were walking out of the store as Vinnie was about to walk in. Separately and together, they were *nice*.

One girl was dressed in a yellow-and-black cheerleader outfit, had the toned body to match, and had shiny blond hair and a pretty face. Her tits weren't world-class, but they were bigger than the tits of any of Vinnie's high-school girlfriends, ten years ago.

The other girl had short black hair, and Vinnie didn't like short hair. But her top and jeans were shaped to show off her figure, and she had a *great* figure. For one thing, Black-Hair Girl had even bigger tits than her cheerleader friend had.

Vinnie thought, *It's time to test-drive my second wish.* Aloud, Vinnie said, "You are mine."

Vinnie expected that both girls would immediately declare their love and would offer their bodies. Instead, what happened was—

The cheerleader said, " 'You are mine'? In your dreams."

Black-Hair Girl said, "You're, what, in your thirties, loser? We don't date old men."

Vinnie was confused. "Maybe you didn't hear me. *You are mine.*"

Black-Hair Girl said, "O-o-kay, you're creeping us out."

Cheerleader said, "I have pepper spray in my purse." She started rummaging through that purse.

"I don't have pepper spray," said Black-Hair Girl, "but I have something even better." She pulled out a smartphone and held it up. "Smile for the camera, mister."

"Now leave us alone," Cheerleader added.

"Give me that," Vinnie said, grabbing the smartphone out of Black-Haired Girl's hand. He was about to throw the smartphone down hard on the parking-lot pavement—

—but now Cheerleader was pointing a pepper-spray bottle at Vinnie. Not to mention, a frowning couple in their fifties was watching the show.

Vinnie gave Black-Hair Girl her smartphone back, then rushed past the two young hotties and the older couple to enter the supermarket.

****

Once Vinnie got home, he didn't even take time to unload groceries. He went straight to the lamp, then Vinnie *slapped* the lamp.

After Kharmesh blue-smoked, Vinnie demanded, "What the fuck kind of trick did you pull on me? My second wish didn't work!"

Kharmesh just grinned. "So, Master, you spoke ye magic words to a girl or girls, but naught did happen?"

"On *neither* girl. And I said 'You are mine' *twice!*"

"Describe ye girls, and how long ago you did converse with them."

Vinnie did so, then Kharmesh made his big crystal ball appear. A few seconds later, Kharmesh said, "Ye yellow-haired girl and ye black-haired girl, are they ye girls of whom you speak?"

"Why aren't they fucking and sucking me right now? Why didn't the magic words work *at all?*"

Kharmesh's deep voice laughed. "Because they be both seventeen, Master. You wished to have this power over 'a woman.' Meaning, an adult female human. But by ye laws of your country, a female human under eighteen is not an adult, she is a child."

"You son of a bitch. So a girl could be *almost* grown up, it's the day before her eighteenth birthday, and my wish won't work on her?"

"Exactly, Master." Kharmesh didn't add *Ha ha, I tricked you, neener-neener*, but the genie's big grin was taunting.

"*Fine*," Vinnie said angrily. "Back in your lamp, blue boy."

Just before Kharmesh blue-smoked, he frowned. Vinnie assumed this was because of Vinnie's schoolyard insult.

****

Vinnie decided that since he could magically get any (adult) woman he wanted for sex, he would start with a woman whom he never, ever could get nonmagically.

There was a bar in downtown Boston that Vinnie had heard about, but never been in: The Blue Star Lounge. It was for people with lots and lots of money—

The place had a twenty-dollar cover charge (in addition to the two-drink minimum); and not only did men have to wear a coat and tie to get in, but the outfit couldn't look cheap.

The payoff for the men who could afford their way inside was that the women in the Blue Star Lounge were dick-hardening gorgeous.

So Vinnie passed up the outfit that he wore as a "wholesale meat salesman," and put on the suit that he wore only for funerals. Then he got in his car and drove downtown.

When he walked in, he saw that almost every woman there was being talked-to by at least one guy. And just as Vinnie had heard, every one of those women was worthy of male attention. He saw lots of blondes and redheads, many beautiful faces and sleek shapes, and every woman had bigger-than-average tits.

But among this roomful of hit-on hotties, two beauties were alone. Each sat at opposite ends of the main bar, and each sipped an expensive drink.

At the right end of the bar was a muscle-toned babe whose brunette hair was piled up on her head. She was dressed in white, and her ears hosted dangling diamond earrings. She had tan skin; the white clothing and white earrings made her look strange and mysterious.

At the left end of the bar was a big-breasted blonde, who was wearing a tight, light-purple dress. Vinnie could tell at a glance that everything about her that could be faked, was—

Her long, blonde hair was too perfectly colored, her fingernails were too long and too perfectly shaped, and she had big, puffy, cocksucker lips.

Not to mention, the size of her tits was ridiculous; hers was even bigger than the green-eyed genie's tits.

For Vinnie, the answer to "Which woman do I love-whammy?" was obvious.

****

"Hello," Vinnie said to the blonde, "I'm Vincent. But call me *Vinnie*."

She looked Vinnie up and down. Her eyes stopped at his tie, which had a tiny tomato-sauce stain. She said, "I'd like to be alone now," and turned away to face the bar mirror.

Vinnie said, "You are mine."

She turned back to face him, and her expression was completely different. "Hello, Vincent, I'm Lola. Oh god, my working name is Lola; my real name is Cheryl. I love you."

Whoa, it really works, Vinnie thought. Aloud he asked her, " 'Working name'? Are you a *whore*, Cheryl?"

"Yes, I am," she said nervously. "Is that all right?"

"Depends. You gonna fuck and suck me for free, or you gonna charge me for it?"

"*For free*, darling! And it'll be the best fuck I know how to give."

"Great. So whaddaya say we ditch this place?"

"*Pardon me*, sir," said the bartender. "We do have a two-drink minimum, so you can't leave yet. What can I get you?"

Vinnie was about to say *Shove your two-drink minimum up your ass*, but then he noticed the walkie-talkie sitting in a charger behind the bar; and Vinnie recalled how beefy the bouncers were. So Vinnie decided that the smart thing was to play along.

Vinnie bought a Budweiser for himself, and a fruity drink for Cheryl, and the cost made him choke. Vinnie decided that if the Blue Star Lounge was going to become a habit, Vinnie would need to rob a liquor store. (Again.)

****

Some time later, Vinnie and Cheryl were in Vinnie's car, headed back to Cheryl's place.

Vinnie asked, "Do you have a pimp?" Vinnie needed to know if some mook was following him.

Cheryl replied, "No, darling. The only man in my work-life is my lawyer, who will post bail if I get arrested."

Vinnie said nothing more, and he asked Cheryl nothing else. Because really, Vinnie didn't care what Cheryl did, or said, or thought.

****

Vinnie and Cheryl were in Cheryl's apartment (her real apartment, not her "working" apartment). The furniture was expensive, the TV was huge, and the artwork on the walls looked classy.

But looking at paintings was not why Vinnie was there. "Okay, Cheryl, let's see you strip."

"As you wish, darling," Cheryl replied.

The striptease was amazing. Her body was toned, and so didn't jiggle at all, except for her ass and tits. She was wearing a no-shit garter belt and stockings, which Vinnie had never seen outside of porn movies.

When she took her purple bra off, those humongous tits of hers jiggled and *jiggled.*

He reached for her tits. In a strip club, such a move would make the stripper smile but move away; but Cheryl now danced *toward* Vinnie.

"Oh yes, darling," she cooed, "I want you to feel my tits if that's what you want."

Vinnie stroked her tits, then he slurped on her nipples. "*Mmm,*" Cheryl said. "That feels so good, darling."

When Cheryl shimmied her panties off, Vinnie discovered that her public hair was trimmed into a heart shape. Her pussy lips were puffy, and she reeked of arousal.

She wasn't the only one who was aroused.

Cheryl noticed. "Would you like me to do something about your hard-on, Vincent darling?"

Vinnie unzipped his fly and fished his cock out of his slacks (with difficulty; he was indeed hard). "Yeah, bitch, show me what you can do with your mouth."

What she could do with her warm, wet mouth was quite a lot, apparently. It seemed only seconds later that he had to fall back onto the couch because he couldn't remain standing.

God, Cheryl's blowjob felt good!

When Vinnie was about to pop, he said "Stop! I want to get undressed."

"Would you like my help, darling? I would love to undress you out of that suit."

"Why? I've been undressing myself since I was four." Women could be so stupid sometimes.

When Vinnie was naked, he said, "Okay, take me to your bedroom."

Cheryl's bedroom, it turned out, was various kinds of light purple.

When Cheryl had one knee on her bed, she looked over her shoulder at Vinnie. "I am *so wet* for you, Vincent darling. I haven't felt like this since I was sixteen."

Sure enough, when Vinnie stuck his dick into Cheryl's pussy, he couldn't believe how *wet* she was. That part of the fucking was really nice.

But Cheryl scratching his back and screaming, those things were distracting.

"Oh *god*, Vincent, I love you, I love you fucking me, I'm *comiiiiiing!*"

Vinnie's ears hurt.

****

When Vinnie was dressed again in his funeral suit, he looked at Cheryl, who was still naked in bed. He said, "How about I'm your pimp from now on? Three-fourths of what you earn, you give to me."

"Whatever you want, darling. Thank you, Vincent, for letting me keep a quarter."

"So I guess I need to know how to contact you now."

Cheryl's face lit up. "Vincent darling, you're asking for my *telephone number?*"

Chapter 13
"Be Blind!"

Wednesday, July 23, evening
Bambino's Restaurant, Boston, Massachusetts

Tony and his boys were eating dinner in an Italian restaurant, and Vinnie hated being there.

Not because of the expense. Tony paid for the rental of a private room, and paid for everyone's meal. He also threw in a generous tip for the waiters.

Still, the meal wasn't completely free. Tony expected every one of his boys to add their own tip to the check that they weren't paying for. That was only an annoyance.

No, Vinnie hated being here because:

One, it meant socializing with Tony's boys, and Vinnie spent enough time with Tony's other boys as it was.

Two, Vinnie had to sit here and listen to Cesare Sangiorgi brown-nose Tony all night.

Tony's great-whatever grandfathers came from Sicily. Cesare was likewise Sicilian. Cesare was trying to play up his Sicilianness, to become Tony's favorite. Whereas Vinnie's people had come from northern Italy, not anywhere close to Sicily, so he couldn't compete with Cesare in that regard.

Tony was speaking: "I had a friend, until recently. I *trusted* him, I thought he was a man of honor."

"Honor is good," agreed Cesare.

"I loaned him money. The agreement was, my friend would buy teddy bears, sell them at a profit, and pay back my loan with a fair interest."

"That was a smart idea," said Cesare. "You always spot the smart deals, Tony."

"I found out my friend bought the teddy bears. My friend sold the teddy bears. But did he pay me back? *No*. Worse, he started telling me sad stories."

"He should have respected you, Tony," Cesare said. "You deserve respect."

Maybe so, maybe not. Vinnie remembered seeing bricks of white powder, all wrapped in plastic—they looked nothing like teddy bears. But now Vinnie kept his mouth shut.

Tony continued, "He dishonored this Family. He dishonored *me*. So I sent Vinnie to talk to him. Vinnie, did you give him my message? About honor?"

Vinnie looked at everyone looking back at him. He liked that Tony had entrusted this job to *him*, not to Cesare. "I said to him, quote, Sometimes it costs a man to keep his honor. But always it costs a man more to lose his honor, unquote."

"You did good, Vinnie," Tony said. "You took care of the problem."

Vinnie, was smiling, basking in Tony's approval—

Then Cesare said, "Well, those Alps Italians, they have their uses. Even if their ancestors *were* almost German."

Vinnie said, "Whereas if he'd sent *you*, Sangiorgi, youda been whistling *The Godfather* song and alerted the mook's entire neighborhood. You got no *brains*; we all know this."

"Boys, stop arguing," Tony said. "I want to enjoy my dinner."

****

An hour later, the private dinner had broken up. The first thing Vinnie had done (after leaving a five-dollar tip on the table) was to dash off to the men's can.

What he did next, it took some time doing.

When he finally got out to the parking lot, everyone was gone except for Tony and Cesare. Tony was standing by his open car door; Cesare was talking earnestly to Tony, and had his hand on the older man's shoulder.

Vinnie thought, *Cesare, I bet if Tony told you to suck his dick here in the parking lot, you'd do it with a smile.*

Then Tony shook hands with Cesare, got in his car, and drove off. Tony's car passed close to Vinnie; Vinnie waved.

By now, Cesare was walking across the restaurant's parking lot. Vinnie yelled, "HEY, YOU! YES, YOU, THE SICILIAN SUCK-DICK! STOP RIGHT THERE!"

****

Vinnie got in Cesare's face. "What's the fucking idea of trash-talking me right after Tony was talking me up to the other fellas, huh? Are you jealous because when Tony needed a job done, he sent *me* and not *you?*"

"*Me*, jealous of *you*, Lavagetto? I'm Sicilian—we're jealous of nobody. Especially nobody from northern Italy."

Vinnie sneered. "Tony has announced that soon he'll induct someone," make the guy be a full member of the Family. "You really think he's gonna induct a guy who does nothing besides tell Tony he's smart, and he's gonna pass up a guy who solves problems for him?"

"Yeah, because we Sicilians stick together. You watch, soon I'll be inducted, while you'll be outside looking in."

The "discussion" continued. Vinnie called Cesare nasty names; meanwhile, Cesare was rudely insulting Vinnie. Each man got the idea of drawing down on the other at the same moment.

Staring down the barrel of Cesare's gun, Vinnie thought, *I might die now. And what a waste, after I found the genie lamp—The blindness wish, I forgot all about it!*

Vinnie looked into Cesare's eyes and said, "Be blind."

Cesare's cockiness vanished instantly. "WHAT THE FUCK? I CAN'T SEE!"

Vinnie was taking aim, but then blind Cesare started waving his gun around. Even as the trained-killer part of Vinnie's brain was pulling the trigger on his silenced pistol, part of his brain was telling him to jump to the right.

Thyoo/BANG!

Fuck it, fuck, this hurts! Vinnie thought. Cesare's shot had grazed his left arm. On the other hand, Vinnie had put a bullet into Cesare's stomach.

Which meant that Cesare would die *eventually.* Vinnie decided—

Thyoo.

—to help Mother Nature along.

For Vinnie, getting his car keys out of his left pants pocket was a slow, agonizing process. During which, he dripped blood on the pavement.

Vinnie had watched enough cop shows to know what that meant. *Murder evidence!*

Somehow Vinnie got into his car, and shut the door. He grabbed the folded-up blanket that he kept on the back seat, and manhandled the blanket so that it was between his bleeding left arm and the closed car door.

Somehow, Vinnie managed to drive home.

Somehow, Vinnie managed to get the garage door shut, and get into his house.

Somehow, Vinnie managed to stumble into his bedroom.

After some trouble, Vinnie rubbed the lamp. Kharmesh appeared.

Kharmesh looked at Vinnie's bleeding arm and *smiled.* "Master, you have a problem."

Chapter 14
Each Squeezes The Other

"I have a *problem?*" Vinnie said. "No shit, Sherlock! Don't stand there, heal me!"

Kharmesh still was grinning. "I am not required to."

"What does *that* mean?"

"I must needs grant your three wishes. I have done so. What you ask for now is a magical *request.* I am not required to grant your magical requests."

"So you're refusing to heal my motherfucking arm?"

Kharmesh's smile got bigger. "Exactly, Master. I will not heal you, unless. . ."

"Unless *what?*" he asked, panting.

Vinnie now was feeling lightheaded from blood loss.

Still grinning, Kharmesh said, "That slut Fatima is allowed to stay out of her lamp. I want ye same thing."

"And if I say no?"

"Then I hope you know a barber who will treat your wound, who will also keep a quiet tongue. If not, 'tis to ye gaol for you. And from gaol, mayhap ye gallows, hm?"

The words were on the tip of Vinnie's tongue: *Anything, I agree to anything, just heal my arm and get rid of all the evidence—*

Then Vinnie remembered that movie line about "Make him an offer he can't refuse." Kharmesh, that blue-skinned bastard, was *squeezing* Vinnie!

Vinnie didn't think things through, he was simply pissed that Kharmesh was disrespecting him: "Get the fuck back in your motherfucking lamp."

Kharmesh's cruel grin turned into a face of fear. Then he blue-smoked.

****

Vinnie thought, *What just happened?* Why did the genie look so *scared* at being told, in effect, "Go to your room, boy"?

It was hard to think now. Vinnie was still feeling lightheaded from the blood loss, his tongue felt as dry as sandpaper, and his arm *hurt*. But he needed to figure this out.

Vinnie realized that he needed an edge on Kharmesh, but right then, the genie sure as hell had an edge on *him*. The trouble was, what did he know about Kharmesh, or genies in general, that Vinnie could use against Kharmesh?

Then Vinnie remembered something that the other genie had said, and this gave him hope.

Vinnie rubbed the lamp again. (He had to do it one-handed, holding the lamp between his knees.) When Kharmesh came out, the genie said, "You still bleed. Alas, poor Master."

"Shut up. The genie bitch said to me, 'Since you're *not* my master, I don't have to tell you jack shit.' Does that mean if I ask you a question, you have to answer?"

Kharmesh frowned. "Yes, Master, I must needs answer your question."

"Can you lie to me?"

The genie's face was devoid of expression. "No, Master."

"So I can believe whatever you tell me?"

Kharmesh smiled. "It certainly sounds that way, does it not?"

"Now you're acting tricky. Back in your lamp, asswipe."

Kharmesh had time enough to slump his shoulders before he blue-smoked.

Vinnie let Kharmesh stew for five minutes before rubbing the lamp again.

Those five minutes were as hard on Vinnie as they were of Kharmesh, Vinnie was sure. Vinnie felt awful, and who knew what the cops were planning?

Vinnie had just rubbed the lamp; Kharmesh came out of the lamp for the third time that evening. Vinnie demanded, "How can I be sure when you tell me something, that it's honest truth and not bullshit?"

Kharmesh, looking worried, told him.

Then Vinnie said, "Tell me the truth, Why does going back in your lamp gets you scared?"

Kharmesh fussed about being called *scared*. He tried to evade answering the question, but Vinnie didn't let up.

Eventually Kharmesh said, "Because I know not when I will come out again."

In further back-and-forth questioning, Vinnie found out that:

Just before a genie-master dies, he is compelled to either give the lamp to someone he trusts, or else to hide the lamp where theoretically nobody will find it. The lamp always does get found, but not until decades or even centuries later. This last time, for instance, Kharmesh was stuck in his lamp for 272 years. Since a Vessel cannot be found by human magic, *djinn* magic, or satanic magic, the only way to find Kharmesh's lamp is to stumble upon it. So every time Kharmesh gets sent into his lamp, he expects to not be out of his lamp for at least fifty years.

Vinnie said, "I got it now. So tell me *exactly* what you want."

"To be out of the lamp for as long as you live."

"That's dumb. I could be dead tomorrow."

"No, such is unlikely." Then Kharmesh made his big glass ball appear, and worked it. "Your Date Of Fated Death is July 14, 2034."

"I'm gonna die when I'm *forty-six?* What do I die of?"

"I cannot say, Master. Mayhap you will die after a long bout of Coughing Sickness, or mayhap you will be thrown from a horse and snap your neck."

"Or maybe I'll get shot." Then Vinnie remembered something else he'd been told this morning: "If you're with me, you have to protect me, right?"

Kharmesh still was working his glass ball. "I see that you have killed a man: Cesare Sangiorgi. His murder is being investigated. Why do the watchmen wear gloves, I wonder. Master, you have many problems now."

Only then did the genie answer Vinnie's question: "Yes, if I am with you, I must needs protect you." Then he added, "I might need to protect you from ye watchmen soon."

Vinnie replied, "Yeah, yeah, you're trying to get me to agree to your deal. You think I can't spot a hustle? But okay, you want to stay out of the lamp? On four conditions."

"*Four*, Master?"

"You heal me, and you clean up all the evidence that links Cesare's murder to me. You act as my bodyguard, since you gotta do that anyway. And you do whatever you need to do, so you don't seem like a blue-skinned guy who talks funny."

"I am of the Blue Tribe! We are proud of how we look."

"I don't give a rat's ass. Listen, pal, the time for horse-trading is *over!* Do you give me what I want, in return you get what you want? Or do I get my shovel out of the garage and bury your lamp in as deep a hole as I can dig? With you inside the lamp?"

****

Thus it came to be that Vinnie's arm was magically healed like he was never shot. There came to be no blood in his car, on his clothes, or on his blanket.

The blood-spatter in the Bambino's Restaurant parking lot disappeared (to the confusion of crime-scene investigators). Cesare had been shot twice, but nobody could find the bullets *anywhere*.

Kharmesh didn't tell Vinnie what exactly he'd meant by "If you would that I not 'talk funny,' I must needs touch your forehead." The good news was that, when the process was all done, Kharmesh no longer talked like a Brit. The bad news was that Kharmesh got his new speech by "memory-reading" Vinnie, and Vinnie was forced to relive all the times Papa had beat him.

All that the Family knew is that the next time they saw Vinnie, he had his own bodyguard. A very tall, very muscular, Arab-looking mook who wore sunglasses so black that nobody could tell what color his eyes were. And even though the bodyguard told everyone, "I'm not from around here," and indeed nobody had seen him before, he sounded pure Boston.

Chapter 15
One-Man Army (With Help)

The next morning

Tony was Vinnie's boss in the Family. Tony's cover was as a meat wholesaler, Antonini's Meats. Tony's grandfather had started the business.

Vinnie didn't know what kind of business the grandfather had run, but in Tony's case, not all the blood on the floor of Antonini's Meats was from cows and pigs.

Vinnie walked in wearing slacks, white shirt, and tie. If anybody with a badge asked, Vinnie was one of Tony's salesman. Vinnie even had a desk with phone—but except for a writing pad and two pens, his desk was empty.

But Vinnie wasn't the only one who walked in. Kharmesh actually walked in just before Vinnie did.

"Hey!" Tony yelled. "You! Whoever you are, you gotta use the—"

Vinnie said, "His name's Kharmesh. He's my bodyguard."

Tony said, "Yeah? And how can you afford a bodyguard?"

Vinnie said, "Maybe somebody dumped a million bucks on my bed. I didn't steal nuthin' from you, so don't sweat it."

"Yeah? This is *my* business, Lavagetto, and I say who comes into the employee area! I don't know nuthin' about your guy except he's not Italian and he's not Catholic. He could be goddamn FBI—"

Kharmesh's sunglasses turned toward Tony's face. "Trust me," Kharmesh said.

"—but still, he looks like he has an honest face. He can stay, Lavagetto, but ask me ahead of time, next time."

"Uh, no problem, will do," surprised Vinnie replied.

But before Vinnie could say more, Tony said, "We got a problem. Cesare got whacked last night. The cops think—"

Right then, Vinnie got to find out for himself what the cops thought. A crew-cut man walked in, holding a gold badge aloft. "MAY I HAVE YOUR ATTENTION, PLEASE. I AM DETECTIVE SAM BLOCK, CITY HOMICIDE, HERE TO INVESTIGATE THE MURDER OF CESARE SANGIORGI. PLEASE COOPERATE AND WE WILL BE GONE IN NO TIME FLAT."

Following behind the detective were several uniformed cops and several crime-scene investigators.

****

Detective Block and the other cops interviewed everyone who'd been at Bambino's Restaurant the previous night, but the cops didn't find out a thing. *Omertà* (the code of silence) was very much in force.

So the detective didn't especially notice Vinnie's "I didn't see nothing, I didn't hear nothing," when everyone else was saying the same thing.

That didn't mean that the detective believed Tony or his boys. Everyone who was at Bambino's the previous night, got his car searched by the crime-scene investigators.

For whatever reason, Vinnie and Tony got their cars searched last, and searched more thoroughly. Vinnie (and Kharmesh) were allowed to watch the search of Vinnie's car, but Vinnie wasn't allowed to get close to his car.

Vinnie had to hand his keys to one of the uniformed cops, who opened Vinnie's car completely—front doors, back doors, and trunk. The crime-scene people sprayed something on the driver's seat (bottom and back), the passenger seat (bottom and back), the steering wheel, the trunk lid, and the trunk; then the technicians waved a purple light around.

Vinnie was jumpy, but made himself look only slightly annoyed. It seemed like forever, but only nine minutes passed before the oldest crime-scene tech announced, "It's clean."

Kharmesh turned his sunglasses-covered face toward Vinnie and gave a slight smile.

Then Kharmesh walked over to Detective Block and asked, "What are you looking for?"

Block glared at the disguised genie. "That's police business, buddy, so why even ask?"

Vinnie had followed Kharmesh, curious. Now Vinnie heard Kharmesh say, "Trust me, you can tell me anything. What do you know about the murder?"

Block's anger vanished, and his face relaxed. "Three witnesses, three descriptions of the shooter. The cook swears the shooter was an African-American dwarf, like I can believe that. One witness says the shooter got into a red car, another witness says black, a third witness says the car was white."

Vinnie's car was blue.

Block continued, "All three witnesses say Sangiorgi shot his killer, who then staggered away and drove off. So we're looking for blood in a car."

Kharmesh said, "But you didn't find any blood in any car here, right?"

"Not a drop, no."

Kharmesh said, "Believe me, the fellas here are innocent. These aren't the mooks you're looking for."

Detective Block nodded. Then he yelled, "LET'S WRAP IT UP, PEOPLE. WE'VE WASTED ENOUGH TIME HERE."

Kharmesh, meanwhile, had walked over to Vinnie and had bent down to murmur in Vinnie's ear:

"I've never made a promise to a human before, but the honor of the Blue Tribe demands I keep every word."

****

After the police left, Tony said to Vinnie, "You were the last to leave. Did you see anyone lurking in the parking lot? Hear anybody?"

After all, just because Vinnie had told the police he had seen "nothing" and heard "nothing," didn't mean that nothing had in fact been seen or heard by him.

Vinnie shrugged. "It was dark and I was sleepy. I didn't see nobody but Cesare, and nobody bothered me."

"Well, shit," said Tony.

"What do you think happened?"

"I think they planned to whack *me*, but something went wrong."

"Got any ideas who?" Vinnie asked.

"Yeah, Fyodorov's gang. That drunken Russian hates me."

Vinnie pulled his car keys out of his pocket. "If you think Fyodorov did it, that's good enough for me."

"You planning something? Good, I like a guy who doesn't sit on his ass. How many of the boys will you need?"

"None of 'em," Vinnie said. "Me and Kharmesh will take care of those Russkis."

"By *yourselves?*"

"Don't worry, I know a trick," Vinnie replied. Vinnie waved, and then he and Kharmesh were out the door.

****

Vinnie got behind the wheel of his car; Kharmesh took the passenger seat. Vinnie had driven only a block when Kharmesh ripped off his sunglasses and tossed them on the front dash.

"This stinks on ice," Kharmesh said. "Bad enough I have to obey a human and I have to save a human's life, but what we're doing lacks honor."

"I don't want to hear it."

"Fyodorov didn't whack Sangiorgi, *you* did. If you had honor, you woulda told Tony that."

Vinnie shrugged. "I don't care. I got plans. When those plans work, and I got money and babes and I'm the guy giving the orders, *then* I'll think about honor."

****

Twenty minutes later, Vinnie and Kharmesh arrived near Cossack Imports, which was located in a very old, very ugly industrial part of Boston. Vinnie parked his car a block away.

Cossack Imports turned out to be an old, crappy-looking warehouse. Vinnie saw two doors, one big enough to drive a truck through, and a human-sized door next to it. Guarding the big door were two young men, who each had his hand in a coat pocket. One of the young men was smoking, but he held his cigarette between thumb and index finger, like European men do.

Both door-guards were eyeing big, strong Kharmesh (who was back to wearing sunglasses), and were barely looking at Vinnie. "Can I help you?" the nonsmoker asked, in a thick Russian accent.

"Be blind," Vinnie murmured, quietly enough that the two Russian men couldn't possibly hear him.

Both men brought both hands to their eyes, which meant that neither Russian was holding a gun. Meanwhile, Vinnie was jamming his hand into his own coat, to grab his pistol.

Thyoo. Thyoo. One problem solved.

One guy had yelled something brief in Russian, but Vinnie guessed it translated more to *Hey* or *Shit* than *Guys, everybody come out here right now because we need backup.* In any case, Vinnie stood there for thirty seconds, his gun aimed at the human-sized door, waiting for a bunch of Russian mooks to come bursting out.

When it was obvious that nobody was about to come out, Vinnie asked himself, "Now how do we get through that door?" Because up close, Vinnie saw that the human-sized door had a fish-eye peephole in it.

Vinnie looked over at Kharmesh. "I could use some help getting inside, you know?"

"Fuhgeddaboudit," Kharmesh replied. "All I *have to* do is save your ass, and that is all I *will* do. Getting through the door or not, that's *your* problem."

"And fuck you too," Vinnie replied. Then he decided that if he couldn't use magic to get through that door, and he couldn't use muscles, this left only trickery.

Vinnie pounded on the human-sized door twice with his fist, the way a lazy door guard would. When thirty seconds had passed, with neither the door being opened nor people yelling and gunshots being fired, Vinnie pounded twice on the door again.

Vinnie heard a woman's voice yelling in Russian, then the door was pushed open. The woman who opened the door was about Vinnie's age, and homely. The woman stopped yelling, and looked confused, when she saw Vinnie's face.

Before she did the math and started yelling again, Vinnie—*thyoo*—shot her, pushed her corpse away from him, and stepped through the door.

Kharmesh was right behind Vinnie.

Vinnie and Kharmesh had moved maybe ten feet inside the building when male voices yelled in Russian. Then the shooting began.

Vinnie looked straight down the barrel of the gun of a man on the catwalk. Vinnie saw a muzzle flash. But all Vinnie felt was a momentary puff of air on his face. Right after that, the shooter dropped onto the catwalk.

Meanwhile, a man standing at a table dropped whatever he was doing, in order to scoop up an AK-47. Vinnie didn't give the Russian a chance to fire it; *thyoo.*

Then Vinnie felt the air-puff again, at the same instant he heard gunfire.

Thyoo, thyoo, thyoo. . .

When Vinnie ran out of bullets, he pulled out the empty magazine, dropped it into a coat pocket, pulled a full magazine out of another coat pocket, reloaded, and went back to shooting. Vinnie felt absolutely no fear during those seconds when he was bulletless and fumbling with his gun while mooks were shooting at him.

When everything went silent, Vinnie looked around. The inside of the warehouse was foggy with gunsmoke. Bodies lay everywhere; Pavel Fyodorov was one of those dead bodies. Kharmesh was unhurt, and his face was expressionless.

Vinnie said, "Will you tell me if anyone is still alive?"

Kharmesh paused a second, then said, "Yeah, I'll do that." Kharmesh turned his back on the supposedly dead Russians, summoned his big floating glass ball, and worked it.

Five seconds after he'd started, Kharmesh vanished the glass ball. "There is an injured man on the catwalk"— Kharmesh pointed out where—"and a woman is hiding under her desk in the office."

Vinnie and Kharmesh climbed up the stairs and walked the catwalk. Seconds later, Vinnie was staring into the face of a bleeding man.

"*Nyet!* Please!" the man begged.

Vinnie shot him at point-blank range.

The office turned out to be a building inside the warehouse building. The office's outer walls were inside the warehouse, and the office's unshingled roof was below the warehouse's ceiling. While the guys in the warehouse froze in the winter and baked in the summer, they were watched through big windows by the people in the office, who enjoyed pleasant temperatures for twelve months a year.

Once Vinnie and Kharmesh were in the office, Kharmesh led Vinnie to a particular desk. Vinnie squatted down.

Hiding under the desk was a brunette in her twenties. She looked like the sister of the woman whom Vinnie had shot minutes earlier—the *much hotter* sister of the dead woman.

She whimpered when she saw Vinnie's eyes looking into hers, his silenced pistol held loosely in his right hand. "Pliss—pliss not hurt me," she said.

Vinnie was about to shoot her, till he remembered the *other* magical power he had. He told her, "You are mine," then said, "Come out. What is your name?"

The woman was looking adoringly at him as she came out from under the desk. "I am Ruslana and, and"—she spoke Russian words, then stopped herself. "I love you."

She was wearing a gold wedding ring. Vinnie was glad to know that married women weren't immune to his magic.

Vinnie smiled at her, as Kharmesh rolled his eyes. "Ruslana, I want you to do two things for me."

"Anything! I do anything!"

"First of all, when the police come, I want you to tell them that one man walked around the office, but he didn't see you and you didn't dare come out and look at him."

"I do that," Ruslana promised. "I lie to police."

"The other thing I want from you is for you to pull off your panties. I want to fuck you."

Vinnie fucked her on top of her desk. It was a new experience, banging a babe who talked dirty in Russian.

While Vinnie fucked Ruslana, Kharmesh stood there with arms folded, scowling at the ceiling.

Chapter 16
Inducted And After That

Twenty minutes later

When Vinnie and Kharmesh returned to Antonini's Meats, they found Tony in his office. He had a little TV playing; it was showing live news.

It seemed there had been a shootout at Cossack's Imports, but the Boston Police were being stingy with details.

The news report mentioned that there was "one survivor"; Vinnie saw a quick camera shot of Ruslana, being talked-to by uniforms and detectives. Ruslana was crying buckets.

Nervous Vinnie glanced at Kharmesh.

"Relax," Kharmesh said.

Tony turned off the TV. "You guys did this, by yourselves? *How?* Neither of you even has a scratch!"

Vinnie shrugged. "We got smart, and we used a trick."

"*What trick?*"

"Fuck, Tony, if I told you, it wouldn't be a trick anymore."

Tony looked at Kharmesh. Kharmesh said, "I'm not saying jack shit."

Tony stared into Vinnie's eyes, seemingly forever. Vinnie stared back. Then Tony *smiled*, stood up, and slapped Vinnie on the shoulder.

"Be back here at seven this evening, Lavagetto. You're getting inducted."

When Vinnie and Kharmesh were alone, Kharmesh said, "Tony respects what he thinks you did."

Vinnie replied, "Yeah. And here's what we're gonna do about that."

****

7:00 p.m.
Antonini's Meats, Conference Room

Kharmesh was in a foul mood, even before he stepped out of the car.

A minute later, an older guy whom Vinnie knew only as "Surriento," tried to block Kharmesh from coming into the conference room. Kharmesh spoke a few words to him, and suddenly Kharmesh was Surriento's best pal. (Which had to be because of the genie's magic, because Kharmesh was frowning and acting really unfriendly.)

Likewise, once Vinnie and Kharmesh walked into the conference room, a few other guys bitched about Kharmesh being there, but they shut up once frowning Kharmesh talked to them.

These guys were wise to be cautious: every man in the room was wearing a holster; each holster had a gun in it.

Kharmesh was frisked by two men, who clearly had been frisked often themselves. Kharmesh grumbled, but allowed the frisks; the searchers found no weapons on Kharmesh.

Vinnie was frisked by Tony, who removed the pistol from Vinnie's holster and put the gun in the middle of the table.

The overhead lights were off; lighting came from three candles on the table. By the middle candle were a big, clean ashtray; a "saint card" for the Blessed Virgin; a bottle of white wine from Naples; a corkscrew; and a dagger.

In front of each seat at the table was a wineglass. Tony opened the bottle of wine and poured two fingers' worth of wine into every glass. (Kharmesh covered the wineglass with his big hand and glared at Tony, who glared back but did not pour Kharmesh any wine.)

The men stood and sang "*Il Canto degli Italiani,*" the national anthem of Italy—

Fratelli d'Italia,
l'Italia s'è desta...

Vinnie didn't know the words, so he la-la'd along. Kharmesh didn't bother to pretend.

When the song was finished, Tony said, "Vincent Lavagetto, remain standing."

Then Tony picked up the dagger; Surriento, meanwhile, had picked up the saint card and was fishing something small out of his pocket.

Tony said, "Vincent Lavagetto, do you swear a holy oath that you will put this Family above all other families?"

Vinnie said, "I do."

"Including the family of your birth, and the family that you make by marriage and fatherhood?"

"I do."

"Do you swear a holy oath not to reveal the secrets of this Family to outsiders?"

"I do."

Tony brought the dagger up in front of Vinnie's face, so that Vinnie could see it. Then Tony brought the tip of the dagger down, and nicked Vinnie's lip.

It was only because Vinnie had told Kharmesh ahead of time that he wanted this, that Kharmesh did not now hurt anyone in the room. Kharmesh, did, however, grumble.

Meanwhile, Tony had put the dagger down, and now ran a finger across Vinnie's bleeding lip. Tony wiped his bloodied finger on the saint card that Surriento was holding.

Surriento then revealed a pocket cigarette lighter, which he used to set fire to the saint card.

Surriento handed the burning saint card to Vinnie.

Tony asked, "On pain of eternal hellfire—no hope of Jesus, or salvation, or absolution, or intercession by the

Blessed Mother or any other saint—will you do these acts that you have sworn to do?"

That saint card is sure getting hot!

Vinnie replied, "I will."

Tony glanced at the ashtray and nodded. Wasting no time, Vinnie dropped the burning card into the ashtray. Then Tony said to Vinnie, "By the ritual of blood and fire, and by the holy oaths you have taken, you are now a full member of this Family. We recognize you as a 'man of honor.' "

Kharmesh grunted.

Tony solemnly continued, "You enter this Family only by your choice, and you leave it only by your death. You will protect this Family by gun and knife, and this Family will protect you by gun and knife."

"There is one thing I want to say," Vinnie said, speaking now as solemnly as Tony had spoken.

Vinnie looked into the eyes of every man there. Vinnie looked into one hard face after another, of men who had been Italian-American gangsters for decades.

Then Vinnie said, "Be blind"—

—as he grabbed his pistol off the table, and flicked the safety off.

****

Five minutes later, Vinnie and Kharmesh were in Vinnie's car; Vinnie was driving home.

" 'Man of honor,' my ass," Kharmesh said.

****

The next morning, Vinnie and Kharmesh gathered the boys together. Vinnie explained that the Boston branch of the Family had a new guy in charge.

A few guys gave Vinnie-the-upstart a lot of lip, till Kharmesh walked up to them. Kharmesh didn't say anything and he didn't do anything—he simply stood three inches away from the other fellow, as Kharmesh's frowning face looked down into the other guy's face.

Vinnie was feeling ballsy. He and Kharmesh were having this meeting with "the boys" in the work area of Antonini's Meats, even as crime-scene technicians worked nearby in the conference room, processing the multiple homicides.

Vinnie said next, "You boys have a good thing going now. Start working for me instead of for Tony, and things will stay nice for you. But cross me, you're dead. Those are your choices: be rich or be dead."

Nobody said anything.

"Now show me the books. I want to know what this Family has going with hooking, with gambling, and protection, and loans. . ."

Vinnie thought, *I'm a big shot now. And with Kharmesh saving my ass, nothing is gonna stop me from getting even bigger. Just you watch, world!*

Chapter 17
Return Of The Evil Twins

Friday morning, July 25, 2014
Greentree Lake State Women's Prison

I looked at my watch. I'd been told that Almira and Elvira would be released at nine o'clock this morning; now the time was 10:23.

I wasn't the only one waiting. Michelle Landrieu-LeClerc was splitting her time between looking at her own watch, and glaring at me.

Michelle's feminist glares didn't bother me one bit. Which was only making her angri—

A buzzer blared, announcing the opening of the prison's front door. Almira and Elvira stepped out, wearing the same clothes they'd worn into prison.

"Sorry we're late, Marvin," Almira yelled, as soon as she saw me. "The guards searched our cells before they'd process the paperwork."

"Let them play their chickenshit games one last time," said Elvira, "I don't care. We're *free!*"

Almira walked over to me and kissed me for a *long* time. Only then did she turn toward her parent. "Hello, Mother."

Trust me, tax auditors get greeted more warmly.

Elvira was hanging back, looking first at her twin, then at her mother. Elvira's face looked uncertain.

"We're running late," Michelle said. "Let's get—"

"*Excuse me?*" Elvira said. "We don't see your face for two years, and you think you can show up and boss us around?"

Michelle stabbed a finger in my direction. "You two were dressed up like French-maid sluts, for *him!* I raised you to respect yourself more than that."

"What's your deal, Mother?" said Almira. "I had crack cocaine in my purse. We got caught red-handed. 'I'm still your mother,' you said; you came to our trial and you visited us in jail. But you found out we did something to *please a man*, and you quit visiting the motherfucking prison!"

I spoke up: "Twins, let's change the subject. I'm here to invite you to live with me and work for me. However, there's good news and bad news with that."

"You're a married man," said Michelle. "Does *marriage* mean nothing to you?"

"Says the woman who divorced her husband merely because he was 'stifling' her."

Michelle glared at Almira for telling tales out of school. Almira shrugged.

Almira said to me, "You know I'll live with you, no matter what the bad news is."

Elvira asked, "What's the bad news? And what's the good news?"

I replied, "The good news is: free food and free lodging, now you'll each get the same Shopping Allowance that the other *haremées* get, and you each may leave the mansion, subject to whatever your Parole Officer says. And if you live at the mansion, I'll give you a job with Harper Foundation."

"Hold on," said Elvira, "we each will be in your *harem?* No way, forget—"

"I'd do him for free," said Almira. "Throw in a Shopping Allowance and I'm like, 'We haven't left yet?' "

Michelle said, "Are you two not listening? He is 'offering' to make you his whores!"

"Not true, Michelle," I said, "absolutely not true. Whores just suck and fuck. Fatima will add these two to the work schedule, so they'll also be cooking and pot-scrubbing and toilet-scrubbing."

"On the other hand," Almira said, "if we move back in, we get to fuck you."

I looked straight at Elvira. "If you move back in, you *have to* fuck me. But it's your choice this time, to move in or not."

Elvira looked at her twin. "Almie, I really don't want to live with him."

Almira crossed her arms. "Whereas I really *do* want to live with Marvin. Even if I have to wear that stupid French Maid costume again."

"Oh god, don't remind me. Not to mention, Fatima hates me."

"And whose fault is that, Elvira?" I murmured. Louder, I said, "This time you two won't dress like French Maids."

Michelle scowled. "But they'd *be* French Maids, in every way that counts."

Almira walked up to me and rested a hand on the front of my shirt. "Twin, I'm going with Marvin. If you don't come with us, I will be *upset* with you."

Translation: It would be a while before Elvira was allowed to have sex with her twin sister. Which was what Elvira craved more than anything on the planet.

Elvira wailed, "Almie, don't do this to me!"

Michelle said, "Elvira, you're acting like a child. People get upset with *me* all the time, and *I* don't—"

But Elvira was already walking toward me. Elvira looked over a slumped shoulder and said to Michelle, "I guess we'll see you around, Mother."

Just before the three of us got in my car, I said to Elvira, "When you have sex with me, I will do my damnedest to make it good for you."

"You'd better," she replied.

Almira said, "The flip side, twin, is that *you* better make the sex good for *him.*"

****

As soon as we got in the car, Almira asked, "Is it okay to call you *sir* again?"

"Gag me," Elvira said.

I replied, "Yes, Almira, you may."

Almira smiled into my rear-view mirror. "Thank you, Marvin sir."

Elvira looked back at the retreating prison. "I can't believe they actually paroled us."

I said, "It helped that you both had a clean prison record. Well, except for Almira slugging a woman in the mouth in the laundry room."

Almira said, "That's because Lizzie—wait a minute, how do you know about that?" Almira turned to glare at Elvira. "Thanks for spilling the beans, twin!"

"But I didn't—"

I said, "Don't blame Elvira. I read about it in your prison record."

Elvira said, "The parole board let you read our prison records? Those things are supposed to be confidential."

I replied, "Nah, I found it out from SJ-1. You remember, the tall woman who dresses like a robot—"

"Fatima's lesbian submissive," said Almira. "We remember."

I said, "It turns out that SJ-1 is amazing at hacking. She hacked both your prison records. Elvira, you were a choirgirl in prison."

"Because I knew what Almie would do if I caused problems for us."

****

During the drive to town, Almira said to me, "It is *great* to be able to talk to you for more than an hour a week—"

"Yeah, wonderful," Elvira said without enthusiasm.

"—but there's something I'm dying to know about, and you brushed it off when I asked you back in February."

I blinked. "You remember something we talked about in February?"

"You landing that airplane you were a passenger on. The news made it out to be a big deal—you beat up a hijacker! But when I asked you back in February, you shrugged it off."

****

I told them the story. Then I said to Almira, "Look, it was no big deal. Omaha had to bring in a pilot who was qualified to fly the Boeing 747, and he got on the radio and talked me through landing the plane. I just followed instructions."

It was Elvira, not Almira, who commented: "R-i-ght, like just anyone can land a big-ass airplane, even with someone talking in their ear the whole time."

I was surprised. Elvira had just paid me a compliment. She had never complimented me before.

Chapter 18
Bad News For Elvira

Local office, State Dept. of Prisons, Parole Division

I drove the twins straight to the parole office, so that they could report-in without delay. The twins were unhappy with my decision.

We had to wait half an hour in the waiting room. Finally a black man in his fifties called for Almira and Elvira. The man looked tired, even though it wasn't noon yet.

When the twins stood up, I stood up too. The parole officer shook his head. "Family and friends can't come back here. Sorry, Mr. Harper."

"I'm not their family. I'm here as their landlord, you might say, and as their employer."

"Well. . ."

"How many of your clients *lie* to you with every breath? You want to know the truth, I'll tell you the truth."

The parole officer smiled. " 'Truth.' Yeah, I don't get much of that in this job. Sure, Mister Harper, join us." The parole officer beckoned the three of us toward the back.

"Hold on," said Elvira, not moving. "Are you calling me a liar? You don't know me! I won't put up with this shit."

The parole officer, who had been smiling at me, lost his smile completely. "Lose the attitude, girlie. It's *me* who ain't gone put up with no shit from *you*. I can make your life hell, and the sooner you knows that, the better we works together. Now come on, I ain't got no time to waste."

As we were walking through a room of metal desks, I said, "Please, call me Marvin." I put my hand out.

He replied, "And I'm Mar*tin*, as in 'Dr. King.' Martin Howard." He shook my hand.

As soon as his eyes changed expression and he started to say *I am yours*, I said, "Let's just be friends."

Soon Martin Howard sat down at a metal desk, and motioned us to chairs in front of that desk. At the next desk over, a bottle blonde in her thirties was talking to two black men—one in his twenties, one in his forties.

The younger man was eyeing the twins like a dog would look at a steak. "Hello, mamas, you two be *fine*. What you doing here, and what you gone be doing later?"

The older parolee slapped the younger parolee on the back of his head. "You show some respect! That Marvin Harper with them."

Elvira's look was haughty. "What we're doing here is *none* of your business."

"Please be nice, Elvira," I said.

Almira looked like she was about to act haughty too, but she switched gears: "We just got out of prison, and we're here to tell whoever, where we're living and working."

"What was you be in for?" the younger man asked.

The older man said, "You gots a place to live and a job *already?* Damn."

Almira replied, "Drugs, we were both in for drugs."

I asked the older man, "How long does it take for a parolee to get a place to live and a job? Usually."

He replied, "They could get a place to stay today—if they willing to live in a halfway house. But if they don't want no halfway house, they gots to have money for rent and deposit. Money, that mean a job. But nobody give no job to no ex-con."

"*Nobody?*" I said.

"Unless it be work on the sly. And if the Man, he decide to not pay you no money, what you do? You an ex-con, you can't say shit."

"I know that's right," the younger man agreed.

"Damn," said Elvira.

****

A half-hour later, I stopped the car just outside the gate to the mansion. "Last chance to back out, Elvira."

"If I say no to being in your harem, do I still have a job at the Harper Foundation?"

"Nope. Almira would, you wouldn't."

"Why not? You promised!"

"Because I'm a kind man. And right now, the kindest thing I could do for you is to call you out on your bullshit."

Elvira looked at Almira. "If I went to live with Mother, would you—"

"Not a chance, Elvie!"

****

Two minutes later

Fatima's first words to Elvira were, "If it were up to me, you wouldn't be here. You *wronged* Master."

Then Housekeeper Fatima gave Almira and Elvira their housework assignments.

Almira was assigned to days of pot-scrubbing, alternating with days of food preparation. Almira shrugged.

Elvira's assignment? Cleaning the bathrooms—and my mansion had *lots* of bathrooms.

I was only half-listening. Now it was hitting me that Elvira was one of the few people immune to *djinni* mind control, she was an evil bitch, and I'd brought her into my house. *Again.* I strongly hoped that I would not regret this.

Chapter 19
Elvira Meets Aunt Claire

After Fatima gave Elvira and her sister their work assignments, Fatima said, "Actually, you've come on a very special day. Tonight is one of Master's special affairs."

Almira asked, "What happens tonight?"

Marvin was still standing nearby, so he spoke up: "Dinner in the ballroom. My parents and my Aunt Claire are invited, and any ex-*haremées* in town also might show up."

Elvira rolled her eyes. Dinner with Marvin's relatives and a bunch of former sex-slaves sounded almost as bad as prison.

Anna Kay walked into the kitchen, said, "I'm back," then kissed Marvin like she didn't care who was watching. Elvira looked away.

Anna Kay said, "Twins, welcome back, and welcome to our home. Um, who is who?"

Elvira's sister said, "I'm Almira. Congratulations on your marriage. That's a beautiful ring you're wearing."

Anna Kay and Almira spent a full minute talking like Stepford wives; Elvira said nothing. Marriage was a tool of the Patriarchy, and no way was Elvira going that route unless she called every shot in the marriage.

Anna Kay stopped in mid-sentence, then asked, "You two have anything decent to wear tonight?"

"Just what we're wearing," said Almira.

"Which hasn't been washed in four years," Elvira said.

Marvin said to Anna Kay, "I guess you or I will have to take the twins to their mother's house, so they can empty out their closets."

"No, honey, that's dreadful," Anna Kay replied. "Their clothes are four years out of style. They need to go *shopping*."

Fatima said, "I was expecting them to help with food preparation this afternoon."

Anna Kay and Fatima haggled then, with Marvin agreeing to whatever Anna Kay asked of him. The twins got to shop at only one store (Target), and for only a small amount of time (two hours), but whatever they bought would not be charged against each girl's Shopping Allowance.

Elvira was amazed how much Anna Kay pushed Marvin and Fatima to get the twins a good deal. It was almost as if Anna Kay *cared* about the twins; Elvira rolled her eyes.

****

As Anna Kay was driving the twins to Target, Elvira demanded, "What do you want from us?"

Anna Kay said, "Huh? I don't want anything from you. I'm taking you shopping."

"You're being nice to us. Nobody acts nice to us unless they want something."

Elvira expected Anna Kay to act angry, or defensive. Instead, Marvin's wife laughed loudly. "Honey, remember who you're talking to. I can afford a fur coat easier than you can afford a pair of panties. I'm not trying to get something from you."

"Yeah, right, you're acting nice to us just to be nice."

"Bingo. Marvin tells me all the time that he loves me because I'm nice, and he married me because I'm nice."

Elvira didn't know how to reply to that.

****

That evening
Back at the mansion

"Aunt Claire," Marvin said, "this is Almira LeClerc on your left, and her sister Elvira, on your right. Almira and

Elvira, this is my mother's father's sister, Claire Owens."

The old woman gave the twins a fake smile that actually looked genuine, but Elvira knew better. Then the smiling old face showed puzzlement. "How can you be sure who is who?"

Marvin replied, "When only one of them is smiling, it's always Almira."

Elvira scowled. But she had to admit that, since the night she'd met Marvin at that costume party, she'd done a lot less smiling and Almira had done a lot more.

That bitch Fatima had been standing nearby as Marvin had made introductions. Now she said, "You two are lucky to meet Aunt Claire. She's unique—"

"Rubbish," said the old woman. "I'm sure there are other women in their eighties who've gone hang-gliding over the Grand Canyon."

Fatima said, "On the other hand, Aunt Claire, these are the sisters Master told you about. The twins who just got out of prison together."

Fatima was standing where Old Claire couldn't see her face; now Fatima gave Elvira a cruel smile.

Almira asked, "You go hang-gliding over the Grand Canyon? That's dangerous! And especially at your age."

The old woman smiled fondly. "Honey, four years ago I had cancer. It got worse and worse. When Marvin visited me in the hospital, I looked like I had a week to live."

Marvin nodded. Then oddly, Marvin and Fatima exchanged a look.

Old Claire continued: "But I got better. Now the cancer is gone! Now I do the things I was afraid to try before. Because what's the worst that can happen, dead at the bottom? I'll still have lived four years longer than I thought I would."

****

Right after Old Claire talked about hang-gliding over the Grand Canyon, she looked at Marvin. "I want to talk to these two during dinner. Could you rearrange the seating to make that happen, please?"

Elvira said, "Um. . ."

Marvin said, "No problem, Aunt Claire. I'll tell Anna Kay to make out two more place cards."

"Um. . ."

Elvira just wanted to eat her dinner and not have to talk to anyone (except Almira). Elvira certainly didn't want to talk to Marvin's elderly relative.

But what Elvira wanted, didn't matter. Fifteen minutes later, everyone was seated in the ballroom, and Marvin was seated in the middle of a supertable (six dark-wood tables shoved together, end to end). Anna Kay sat on Marvin's left, Virgilia O'Keefe sat on Anna Kay's left, Old Claire sat on Marvin's right, Marvin's parents sat across the table from him, Almira sat across the table from Old Claire, and Elvira sat to Almira's left.

To Old Claire's right, and across the table from Elvira, was Fatima. Elvira frowned.

Most plates at the supertable didn't have place cards, and so there had been competition between the other dinner guests to get a seat near to Marvin. But, Elvira had noticed, it had been a *friendly* competition. Elvira well knew the difference between one woman's *You're my friend* smile at another woman, and an *Eat shit, bitch* smile, and Elvira hadn't seen one unpleasant smile.

So, Elvira guessed, she should feel honored that she and Almira both had place cards; it meant Elvira and her twin could sit together. But Elvira didn't *feel* honored.

Altogether, Elvira was in a lousy mood. It didn't help that Almira clearly was happier than a pig in shit: ". . .Yesterday about this time, I was eating boring food off a plastic tray. But now, I'm eating roast beef off gold-rimmed china! Marvin, you are so sweet to us. Don't you agree, Elvie?"

"Um. . ."

Old Claire looked at the twins. "So how do you two feel about your time in prison?"

Elvira said, "I hated every fu—every minute of it. Mainly because we didn't deserve to be there."

Almira turned to look at her. "Not true. We broke the law, we got caught, we deserved to go to prison." Almira turned to smile at Marvin. "But Marvin spoke up and got us out."

"Bullshit, twin," Elvira said. "We deserved none of what we got. We got thrown in prison for planning to play a prank."

"A *nasty* prank," Marvin's mother said. "A 'prank' that would have ruined the life of that poor woman whose party you crashed."

"So what?" Elvira said. "She was a stripper, she earned her money by pleasing men. She didn't deserve to be fussed and fawned over by the judge."

The room went silent. Then Fatima gave Elvira a shark-grin across the table. "Great going. You haven't even started work at the Harper Foundation yet, and already you've pissed off the big boss."

Elvira sniffed. "You're cracked, Fatima. Why would Marvin get angry at what I said?"

Virgilia leaned forward and glared at Elvira. "The Harper Foundation is named after Marvin, true. But do you know who runs it now? A year ago, Marvin put *me* in charge, sweetie. Virgilia O'Keefe, former stripper. I'm your boss."

From the other end of the supertable, Sherry Benson said, "Virgie is a *good* boss. She's smart."

Elvira thought of lots of things she wanted to say next, but realized that nobody here would sympathize—not even her twin sister. Elvira leaned back in her chair, frowning, with crossed arms.

Old Claire said to Elvira, "You look like you're feeling picked on. I know that's unpleasant."

"*No shit* it's unpleasant. But why aren't *you* giving me static?"

"Because I look at you and I see a woman who feels lonely and unloved. I see someone who needs a friend."

"I don't need your pity, lady, and I don't need you as a 'friend.'"

Fatima laughed. "Don't worry, Elvira, you're doing a splendid job of making sure you'll have no friends at all. Not *here*, anyway."

Virgilia said, "She *is* Michelle LeClerc's daughter. No surprise, Elvira is a self-righteous, entitled princess."

Before Elvira spoke up, or Almira, Old Claire did: "Virgilia, that was uncalled for."

Virgilia didn't apologize, but she lowered her gaze for a second.

Anna Kay pasted on a smile, and looked up and down the supertable. "This mushroom gravy is *delicious*. My thanks to whoever helped make it."

Some women smiled back at Anna Kay; Elvira wasn't one of them.

Then Old Claire turned to her right. "Fatima, my offer of friendship goes for you too. Whenever you need a friend, call me up."

"Oh, wow," Marvin murmured. Elvira had no idea why.

The old woman was a phony; it was obvious. Elvira glared at Old Claire and said, "If you can *think* of being friends with Fatima, you don't give a rat's ass who your friends are. Stop talking to me, old woman."

Almira murmured, "Twin, sometimes you disappoint me."

****

I watched the byplay between Aunt Claire and Elvira, and I didn't know whether to laugh or cry.

Elvira was selfish and she was suspicious—the woman was always unpleasant to be around, except when Almira ordered her twin to act nice.

On the other hand, Aunt Claire's defining quality was kindness. When she'd found out that Uncle Warren was in the hospital, back in 2010, she'd urged me to visit him, even though Uncle Warren's behavior in the hospital had scandalized everyone else. (He'd been getting blowjobs in his hospital bed from Sherry and Virgilia.) What Aunt Claire had seen then, which nobody else had seen (or had cared about), was that Uncle Warren in the hospital had been lonely. After Uncle Warren had died, Aunt Claire had come to his funeral, even though she wasn't related to him at all, and she had been days from death herself. Because of her kindness, everyone loved Aunt Claire, including me.

So I spent one of my three wishes unselfishly in order to give Aunt Claire 9.7 more years of life, and as much pain-free health as possible. I didn't know at the time that my unselfish wish would gain me three more wishes.

As it turned out, I was the only genie-master ever to achieve this. Aunt Claire was the person to benefit from the one unselfish genie-master's one unselfish wish, so just as I was unique, so Aunt Claire was unique. This was why Fatima treated each of us with much respect.

Chapter 20
I Bed Elvira

It was half an hour after my parents and Aunt Claire had gone home. I was walking along the upstairs hallway toward my bedroom when a door opened up. Elvira stepped out into the hallway. She looked nervous.

"Hey, Marvin, you have a *computer program* schedule when the women here have sex with you?"

"Yeah, so that the sex doesn't get routine and so everybody here gets equal time with me. Well, except for Anna Kay and Fatima, of course."

"Of course," she said. Now Elvira looked even more nervous than a minute earlier.

I couldn't figure out Elvira's reaction—I expected her to discuss my sex life with sneers, not look as jittery as if a mad slasher were lurking around the corner.

Then Elvira asked, "So where are Almie and I on your list?"

"Almira is next to last, and you're last. Then when I make up a new list, you'll be wherever the program puts you. You could be first on the new list."

"So when will be my turn? When is the end of this list?"

I did figuring, then I told her, "Six, seven days from now. Schedule's on the refrigerator, if you need the exact day."

Elvira bit her lip. "Could we do it tonight? Would that mess things up?"

"Not at all," I replied, as I speed-dialed Fatima's cel-phone-that-doesn't-exist. (But that's another story.) I said next, "But I'm surprised that you—hey, Fatima."

I asked Fatima over the phone, "Who's on the Sex Schedule for tonight?"

Fatima has a perfect memory, so she didn't need to walk to the refrigerator. With no pause, Fatima answered, "Poppy's got you tonight."

"I'm switching her and Elvira. Would you tell Poppy, please?"

"You're fucking Elvira *tonight?* Wow, I want to be there when you tell *her* that. She'll explode!"

"Actually, it was Elvira's idea."

"Huh," Fatima replied. "Maybe there's hope for her yet."

****

I spent the next hour with Anna Kay in the upstairs lounge, talking with whomever *haremées* also were hanging out there. Elvira spent the next hour making herself pretty, while Almira scrounged.

Then both twins appeared in the upstairs lounge. Almira said, "Doesn't she look *hot?*"

Elvira's dark-brunette hair was pinned up. She was wearing a sexy dark-blue thing—which didn't quite match her dark-blue eyes, but which did show off her big tits. On her feet, Elvira was wearing navy-blue high-heel pumps. For jewelry, Elvira was wearing dark-blue dangling earrings and a diamond necklace.

Every bit of clothing and jewelry that Elvira was now wearing, I had seen worn by Anna Kay or by one of my *haremées*, but I didn't mention this to Elvira.

Now I smiled at Elvira as I stood up. "I'm going to enjoy this."

Elvira frowned.

Anna Kay said, "Girlfriend, *you* will enjoy it too. I guarantee it."

Elvira looked at Anna Kay in confusion. "But Marvin *hates* me."

****

As soon as I shut the bedroom door, Elvira said, "You already know what I look like naked. I look like Almie, except for three moles in different places." Translation: *You don't need to see me naked.*

I smiled at her. "Even if what you just said is true, I want to see for myself."

Elvira stood there as I undressed her, neither fighting me nor helping me.

I liked Almira's tits; they were large and globular in shape, with pink nipples, but they moved like natural tits (because that is what they were). Now I discovered that I liked twin-Elvira's tits, for the same reasons.

But when I caressed Elvira's nipples, I was surprised to find them soft. A minute later, when I reached a finger into her panties, I found her slit to be dry.

I said, "What can I do to make this better for you?"

She looked surprised. "Why would you want to? I'm at your mercy."

I said, "I don't enjoy it if you're not enjoying it."

She looked at me, surprised again. "You're the first guy to tell me that who wasn't a beta-male wuss."

"I'm not a rapist, Elvira, despite what your mother might have told you—"

"I didn't say you—"

"But neither am I a 'beta-male wuss.' I am an alpha male who wants to protect you and to provide for you because you're in my harem. Sexually, protecting you and providing for you means giving you bunches of orgasms and letting you feel safe enough to be uninhibited."

She bit her lip. "Can I undress you? Almie says your body is incredible."

I smiled and nodded.

She unbuttoned my shirt and removed it. I let her.

She bit her lip when I was naked from the waist up. I smiled at her some more.

She reached out both hands and caressed my chest. Her nipples got hard. "God, it's like touching a warm stone statue," she said. "Except I feel your muscles flex when you move. This is *amazing*."

I smiled at her. And I reacted with more than a smile.

****

Thanks to Fatima's wish-grant back in 2010, my bulge in my pants was truly impressive. Elvira glanced down, then stared. She bit her lip again—

And stepped back. Coldly she said, "This is prostitution. Prostitution is illegal. You can't make me do this if I don't want to."

I was unsurprised that Elvira would go diva on me. Calmly I replied, "I don't care if it is illegal or not. I stated my two requirements—sex and chores—and you agreed to all of that in front of your mother and sister. Now I expect you to do what you promised."

"Or what? You'll beat me up? How like a man."

"Sorry to ruin your fantasies, Elvira, but I don't hit women. But again: Now I expect you to do what you promised to do."

"This is prostitution. I can ask Mother to make some phone calls to City Government, and you'll be arrested. But if you don't bother me about sex, you'll stay out of jail."

I laughed, which earned me Elvira's pissed-off face. I said, "Say I was arrested for something prostitution-related. Then what happens next?"

"Then they try you, convict you, and you go to jail."

"Victoria says it wouldn't be a slam-dunk conviction. But okay, suppose the jury says I'm guilty. Then what? You haven't thought this through, honey."

She frowned at my sarcastic *honey*. "Jail, duh."

"Wrong. I'm the hero billionaire, so they'd let me stay out of jail, pending appeal. And believe me, I *would* appeal. I'd spend a million bucks and go all the way to the Supreme Court, just to beat a few weeks in jail and a several-hundred-dollar fine."

"Yeah, you would, just because of your stupid male pride."

"Ah, but what if I *win?* Because Victoria says that the same logic that allows a woman to get an abortion, also allows her to prostitute herself. If I go to the Supreme Court and I win, every prostitution law in the USA would *die*. All because of you."

"I. . ."

"Once again: I must insist, Elvira, that you uphold your end of the bargain."

Elvira lifted her chin. "And if I still say no? You can't do anything except hit me. And then the other girls would see me walk out of here bloody and bruised. See how often you get a blowjob during dinner after *that!*"

I laughed again, reached into my pants pocket, and took out my wallet. I pulled out two twenties and a ten.

To Elvira I said, "I don't need lawyers and I don't need fists. If you won't do your part, I'll use *this:* fifty bucks cash."

"I am not a whore, Marvin."

"No, you're a felon. As in, 'convicted of a felony.' Which ranks you *below* a whore, since prostitution is only a misdemeanor. Nope, the fifty bucks is for the taxi to send you to Michelle's house. Tonight."

She stared at me. Aghast, she said, "You know that Almie wouldn't come with me."

"Uh-huh, and you would lose your job with the Harper Foundation the instant you got in that taxi. Plus, you would never see Almira except when she chose to visit you."

"*Fuck*," Elvira said.

"Not yet," I replied, "but I'm still hopeful."

Elvira glared at me, as she said, "Fine, I'll fuck you." Then her hands reached out, and she started to unfasten my belt.

****

A minute later, we were both naked, and Elvira was staring. "Fuck, your bottom half is like your top half, even more so. I thought Almie was jerking my chain."

Elvira started caressing my legs and ass. My dick, which had gone soft during our argument, again prepared to party.

Now Elvira was staring at my dick. "I am sure this is the biggest cock I've—"

A comment which was guaranteed to make me even bigger and harder.

Elvira dropped flat onto the master bed. "Fuck me now, before I lose my nerve. Almie says I can—"

"Whoa, hold on," I said. "I'm not ready to fuck you yet."

"Are you kidding me? Your thing is staring at the wall above the headboard."

"I haven't touched you all over yet. After I've explored your skin with my hands, *then* I'll fuck you."

"But I want you to fuck me *now*."

I laughed. "Oh, Elvira, did that line ever work when *a guy* used it on *you?*"

"Of course not."

"Well then, ain't gender equality wonderful?"

"Aggh, you're a bastard."

****

Minutes later, I was caressing Elvira: concentrating on touching all of her skin that I could reach, not only the fun parts. Meanwhile, she was caressing me.

Elvira was *ready*. Jeez, they could smell her in the upstairs lounge, she was so ready.

But I had yet to kiss her, and she had yet to kiss me.

I was just about to kneel between her legs and stick my dick in her pussy when she said, "If you were a real man, you'd fuck me now."

I wagged a finger in her face. "I'm the most real man you'll ever meet. But for trying to play games with my head, I'm going to hold off fucking you."

"Aggh! I'm going to tell Almie what a pain you are."

"Be sure to mention the orgasms. She'll want to compare notes."

"Braggart. Maybe you're holding off because you fear you can't measure up."

"Bingo, you got me. So now I'll hold off even longer."

"*God*, you're driving me nuts, you know that?"

****

The fucking, when it finally happened, was pretty much by the book. I was hard, she was wet, and she screamed and thrashed almost every sweaty second that I fucked her. For my part, I lasted for as long as I did only by working a math problem in my head—

My hard dick sliding in an out of the wet and contracting pussy of an orgasmic woman will *always* pop my popcorn.

Not to mention that Elvira, however I might feel about her as a human being, was an attractive woman with shiny dark-brunette hair, dark-blue eyes, a slim and shapely figure, and great tits. While looking at Elvira naked, it was easy for my dick to get hard and to stay hard.

After the sex, when Elvira's breathing, and mine, both were back to (more-or-less) normal, I kissed her.

After I broke the kiss, she looked at me in confusion. "Why are you kissing me?"

"Welcome to the harem," I said, "and welcome to my house."

Chapter 21
It's Not Enough

SIX WEEKS AFTER VINNIE TOOK OVER TONY'S GANG
Saturday, September 6, 2014
Outside a farmhouse turned Carlino meth lab
Rural Clearfield County, Pennsylvania

It had been a full-blown war of the supergangs: Vinnie's and Joe Carlino's. The barn looked like Swiss cheese, what with all the bullet holes in the wood. A Carlino man lay slumped, his head and arms hanging out from the hayloft, a sniper rifle on the ground below him. Outside the barn, many bodies of men in Vinnie's supergang lay still. Italian, non-Italian, Catholic, non-Catholic, white, black, and Asian, the dead members of Vinnie's supergang were the same in death.

But as badly as Vinnie's supergang had been shot up, they'd given out worse, and not only because Vinnie had magically blinded many Carlino boys. For instance, the farmhouse was completely gone, RPG'd into nothingness.

Now the barn door opened up just enough for a man's arm to be thrust out. The arm waved a dirty white t-shirt around. "WE GIVE UP!" a frightened male voice yelled.

Now it was Vinnie's turn to yell: "HEY YOU GUYS, STOP SHOOTING!"

Gunfire outside the barn instantly silenced.

Now some men in Vinnie's supergang high-fived each other. Kharmesh, however, who was standing four feet away from Vinnie, said nothing and he showed no reaction.

Now to take out the trash. Vinnie yelled to the (surviving) men in the barn: "SEND JOE AND MARIO CARLINO AND

THE REST OF THE BIG BOYS OUT, AND WE WON'T HURT THE REST OF YOU."

Seconds later, five men walked out, each with both hands on his head.

"You know the drill," Vinnie said to Joe Carlino.

"Yeah, I know it," Carlino replied, as all five men knelt. Carlino glared into Vinnie's eyes, then Carlino spit on the ground. "I also know you're just a jumped-up punk."

Vinnie said, "No, I'm a *very lucky* jumped-up punk."

Vinnie deliberately took his time at changing out the empty magazine for a fresh one, just to give Carlino longer to sweat. When that task was done, Vinnie said, "You can't imagine how *fucking* lucky I am."

Then Vinnie put his pistol against the side of Joe Carlino's head and blew his brains out. None of this "shoot the mook in the back of the head" nonsense—Vinnie wanted to see Carlino's face when he died.

Meanwhile, four of Vinnie's lieutenants had stepped behind the four other Carlino-supergang bigwigs. *BANG!* Those other guys hadn't been disrespectful to Vinnie, so they got the traditional bullet in the back of the head.

Vinnie left the corpses on the ground, and walked up to the barn. When he got close, he yelled, "YOU GUYS OPEN UP THE BARN AND COME OUT, AND I'LL TELL YOU HOW THINGS ARE GONNA BE."

The barn doors opened up. Some people walked out, some staggered out, and some people needed to be helped out by a buddy. Most of the defeated gangsters were weaponless, but a few dumbshits had guns, which they were pointing up at the sky or down at the ground.

Vinnie said, "You clowns have five seconds to put your guns on the ground, or you die right here."

The dumbasses bent down to lay their guns on the ground. Then suddenly Vinnie's hand and arm came up, magically controlled by Kharmesh.

BANG!

Vinnie turned his face to where his gun-holding hand was pointing. One of Carlino's guys had bent down, like he was going to lay his gun on the ground; but then he'd flipped the barrel of his gun up, and fired his gun.

Vinnie now was looking straight down the barrel of that guy's just-fired gun. At the same moment, Vinnie felt a breeze on his face.

Meaning that, if not for Kharmesh's magical protection, the mook would have shot Vinnie in the face.

"You missed," Vinnie said calmly.

BANG! Vinnie's own gun fired, his hand magically controlled by Kharmesh.

The mook fell back, shot in the middle of his forehead. Of course he was dead before he hit the ground.

The way everyone else saw it, the guy had shot at Vinnie, he'd had the bad luck to miss, and then Vinnie's own lightning-fast reflexes and deadly aim had killed the man before he could fire again. But, so far as witnesses could tell, Vinnie's big bodyguard had just stood there while both guns had fired, and hadn't lifted a finger.

Vinnie now wanted to scream. His own boys were grinning at him, the Carlino boys were looking at him in fear, but he deserved none of it. He, Vincent Lavagetto, hadn't bested the Carlino guy, that had all been Kharmesh's doing.

Vinnie tried to ignore his blue mood. Calmly he looked around at Carlino's defeated gangsters and said, "Here are the new rules. To start with, your percentages don't go to Joe Carlino anymore, they go to me. . . ."

****

Joe Carlino had kept his account books hidden under the cushions of the back seat of his car. Or at least, Vinnie's big bodyguard Kharmesh had found the books there.

Now Vinnie was in the barn, looking at Carlino's account books, as surviving members of Carlino's supergang stood around nervously.

Vinnie slapped the workbench where he was sitting. "This guy Carlino was a total dumbass. For the number of mooks he had working for him, he should have been making more money than this."

A man named Scarlini replied, "Blame that guy Harper. He'd fly out to one of our cities, walk up to some guy who was about to lose his house, and tell the guy he was paying off the guy's entire mortgage. So would the guy borrow from one of our lenders? No. Plus Harper would walk around downtown, walk up to streetwalkers, and ask if they wanted to go home. If a girl said yes, he'd put her on a bus. If her pimp tried to stop her, Harper would beat the guy up. So we been making less money at loan-sharking and at the sex trade, all because of Marvin Harper."

Vinnie said, "Fuck that do-gooder asshole."

"And his housekeeper," Kharmesh muttered.

****

Vinnie was driving back to Boston. He and Kharmesh were alone in the car.

Vinnie spoke into the silence: "Do you genies get bored? You guys live forever, so I figure you get bored a lot."

"Sometimes," Kharmesh said. "When I was a free *djinni*. Almost all the time, as a bound *djinni*—getting stuck inside the lamp is nothing but boring."

Then Kharmesh turned to look at Vinnie. "Why you asking me this? Are *you* bored?"

"No, not bored. It's—I'm the head badass in seven and a half states, and I've got those Sicilian goombahs in New York City surrounded. No reason to think my *impero* won't get bigger and bigger. So I should be walking on air, right?"

Kharmesh shrugged. "I suppose."

"Even Al Capone never did what I've done. But it feels like shit, because only mooks and *jamokes* respect what I've done. Hell, mooks are the only guys who even heard of me."

Kharmesh said, "Oh, well. 'Life's a bitch,' they say."

"Yeah. But I got three wishes granted—how can life be a bitch after *that?*"

****

Vinnie had stopped for a bite to eat in a little town in northeast Pennsylvania. Outside the restaurant was a display case that sold newspapers.

The headline read, "SENATOR CALLS DEMS 'COWARDS SINCE 1968.' "

Vinnie squatted down to read what of the front page that he could see. Apparently a U. S. senator, "Happy Larry" Lawrence from Kentucky, was trash-talking his opponent's party, the Democrats. While it was true that Lawrence was running for re-election in November of 2014, political experts also saw Lawrence's statements as jockeying for the Republican presidential nomination in 2016.

After Vinnie quit reading, he stood up and then pointed to the headline. Vinnie said to Kharmesh, "*This* is what I'm talking about. This bastard might be just as much a crook as I am, but *he* gets headlines, and *he* can run for president! *I* want to be president someday."

Kharmesh shrugged. "And *I* want to be a free *djinni*. You can't become president—not using the lamp, anyway."

"No shit," Vinnie snapped.

****

Vinnie had been quiet all through the meal. When Vinnie and Kharmesh got back in the car, Vinnie immediately grabbed the big road-atlas book and started looking through its pages.

After a few minutes, Vinnie tossed the road atlas to the back seat and pulled out his smartphone. Vinnie told the guy who answered, "Change of plan. Tell the boys, me 'n' Kharmesh are going down to Louisville, Kentucky. . . .No, I don't need anybody else with me."

After Vinnie ended the call, Kharmesh asked, "What are you up to?"

"That senator, Lawrence, he lives in Louisville. I'm gonna get him elected president—making damn sure he knows it was *me* who got him there. If I can't be president, I'll settle for being the guy who pulls the president's strings."

Chapter 22
Vinnie Campaigns For A Senator

One week later
At a campaign rally in Owensboro, Kentucky

Vinnie wasn't smart, and he was a high-school dropout besides, but even he knew that telling Senator Lawrence his real name would just get Vinnie bounced on his ass. So Vinnie had introduced himself as "Vincent Vega."

Not that it had made a difference.

Senator Lawrence had been skeptical that "Vincent Vega" could help him get elected president. In fact, he'd looked at Vinnie like Vinnie were crazy.

The senator had given Vinnie *one* chance: to speak at *one* rally during Lawrence's 2014 re-election campaign. If Vinnie couldn't "make the magic happen" (Happy Larry's words), he'd be given a handshake and sent home.

Kharmesh said he was surprised that Vinnie had been offered even that much.

Now Vinnie and Kharmesh were in Owensboro. Owensboro's population of sixty thousand made it either a very big town or a very small city. In any case, Owensboro was completely different from Boston.

For one thing, everyone here talked like Southerners. For another thing, they liked different music here—who in Boston listened to bluegrass music?—and they ate different foods. Vinnie had a take-it-or-leave-it attitude toward barbeque, whereas Owensboroans *loved* the stuff.

Anyway, here Vinnie was in this strange place, surrounded by these strange people whom he was about to make a speech to. Vinnie was looking at his notecards over and over, but that didn't stop his nervousness.

For one thing, as Vinnie looked out over the crowd, he remembered one of the big reasons he'd been glad to leave school: He'd *hated* giving presentations in front of the class. But now, instead of thirty kids and a teacher, he'd be speaking to hundreds of people now. Or was it thousands?

Now the music ended (by the second bluegrass band of the day), and then the mayor of Owensboro walked to the microphone. "That was the Daviess County Pickers, let's give 'em a big round, y'all. . . .Happy Larry will be up here in a moment. But first, I've got Vincent Vega to talk to you, all the way from Boston. I'm not sure what he's fixing to say, except it'll be about why you should re-elect Happy Larry."

The mayor stepped aside, and Vinnie walked to the microphone. It felt as if he were walking to a noose.

The crowd was silent as they stared at him.

"Hi, you guys, I'm Vincent Vega, and I'm—"

People were frowning, and Vinnie hadn't spoken even a full sentence yet. *Why?*

Then Vinnie realized: If t*heir* accent sounded strange to *him*, then *he* had to sound just as strange to *them*. And Bostonians probably weren't loved here in Owensboro.

"—from Boston. Hey, I'm sorry I missed you guys' big barbecue cookout, but if you're ever in Boston, I'll treat you to some Boston baked beans."

The silence from the crowd remained, but now there were many more frowns. An old man glanced at his watch.

Vinnie ran through the speech, and it really did feel as if Vinnie were the guest of honor at a hanging. He covered topics that Happy Larry's campaign staff had suggested—the national economy; jobs in Kentucky; environmental regulation of coal mines; and the liberal idiocy of the

Democratic challenger, Jerry Hiatt—but nothing Vinnie said got rid of the frowns and silence of the crowd.

Finally he thought, *Fuck this shit. Hit these yahoos with my magical secret weapon.*

Aloud, Vinnie said, "I care about this country. Men of Owensboro—"

Vinnie opened his arms wide.

"—come be my friend. Ladies of Owensboro—"

Vinnie still had his arms stretched wide.

"—*you are mine.* Help me get Happy Larry re-elected."

There was a collective feminine gasp. Women's looks at Vinnie instantly changed from boredom, annoyance, or contempt, to adoration.

Holy shit, it worked!

A woman in the front row asked, "What do you want us to do?"

"Vote for Happy Larry in November. And, uh. . ."

Vinnie had no idea what else to say.

The mayor of Owensboro suggested, "He always can use campaign donations."

"Right," Vinnie replied, feeling relieved.

Vinnie continued, "Folks, there are tables behind you where they're selling t-shirts and taking donations. Give those guys ten bucks. Buy a t-shirt too, if you can afford it."

As one, every female in the crowd (except for little girls and high-school girls) turned around and moved to the tables in the back.

The men in the crowd weren't looking at Vinnie, they were too busy staring flabbergasted at their womenfolk.

Within one minute, the donations/swag tables behind the crowd were doing a booming business.

By the time that Happy Larry finished his speech, most of the women in the crowd were wearing dark-blue-and-two-tone-green "Re-elect Happy Larry to the U.S. Senate" t-shirts.

Later, when Senator Lawrence and Vinnie could talk privately, the senator said, "I'd be a damned fool to send you packing after what you did today. Glad to have you as part of the team, Mr. Vega."

Vinnie replied, "I'm glad to be part of your team, *Mr. President.*"

Lawrence's eyes opened wide.

Chapter 23
I Meet With A Senator

THIRTY-EIGHT DAYS AFTER "VINCENT VEGA" CAMPAIGNED IN OWENSBORO, KENTUCKY
Tuesday, October 21, 2014

I had been surprised and puzzled when Senator "Happy Larry" Lawrence called me up and asked to meet with me. After all, he was a Republican U.S. senator from Kentucky, and I didn't live in Kentucky. But I had no reason *not* to meet with him, so I said, "Sure, come on over."

Kelly Brown and Fatima met Senator Lawrence at our city's tiny airport; thirty minutes later, he and I were facing each other in my man-cave, the mansion's computer room.

Oddly, he'd requested that nobody sit in on our meeting, not even my wife. I didn't argue to bring Anna Kay in; but I argued for Fatima, because she was loyal and discreet. Nope, Senator Lawrence said no to Fatima, too.

So now I gestured for him to take a seat on my couch, I walked to the door and shut it, then I walked behind my desk and sat in my comfortable computer chair.

"What can I do for you, Senator Lawrence?" I asked.

His hearty smile to me looked genuine. "Please, Marvin, call me Larry. Because I think we're going to be good friends."

"That remains to be seen, depending on what happens next, *senator*."

The senator had been carrying a briefcase; now he unlocked it. He held up a magazine. He said, "You recognize this, I'm sure."

I nodded. "The August 2011 issue of *Playboy*. That's Anna Kay, Sherry, me, Olivia, and Virgilia on the cover."

Happy Larry frowned. "The cover caption reads, 'The New Hugh Hefner?' That doesn't bother you?"

"Not really. People have been calling me that since they found out about my *haremées*. That's why Christie Hefner did my Playboy Interview—she's the only person on the planet who would know whether I was like Hugh Hefner or not."

"But having all those women, living with them and fu— enjoying sexual relations with them, surely you can see it's disrespectful to Anna Kay."

"But Anna Kay doesn't feel disrespected. She said as much in *Playboy*, if you'd reread the sidebar-interview that Christie Hefner did with her. In fact nowadays, when a *haremée* has a birthday, Anna Kay bakes her a cake. You'd be surprised how often this makes the girl cry."

"Your wife bakes a cake for a girl who is committing adultery with her husband. *Really?*"

"Anyway, Anna Kay never once has told me, before or after we married, 'You have to kick those girls out.'"

Then I put my elbows on the computer desk, and looked intently at Happy Larry. "Is there a point to mentioning my Playboy Interview and my relationship with Anna Kay?"

"Marvin, I'm here to give you an opportunity to prove that you're not the adulterous deviant that many family-values people in America think you are."

"You're giving me an *opportunity*," I repeated.

Happy Larry gave me a photogenic smile. "Now me, I don't think you're a deviant—but a lot of people I talk to, think you set a bad example for our nation's youth."

"I don't think I'm a deviant at all," I said, laughing. "Take Kelly Brown, the woman who drove you here from the airport. I've paid for her college, I've retained her as my stockbroker, and I often invite her to dinner at the mansion—but she's never lived here, and I've never had any kind of sex with her."

I didn't mention that Kelly Brown was a recovering sexaholic, and *not* having sex with her was the kindest thing I could do for her.

Happy Larry now looked at me skeptically. "I find it hard to believe, having met the young woman, that you haven't had sex with her."

"Those are bodacious ta-tas that she's got, aren't they? And all natural. But believe me or don't believe me about the no-sex, it's true."

Then I looked at the senator again. "You mentioned that you were here to offer me an 'opportunity.' "

The senator leaned forward. "Marvin, my election's November 4th. I'm polling 76 percent among Kentucky women voters, so I think I'm gonna win. Anyway, I'm giving you the opportunity to show that you support family values, by contributing a million dollars to my Senate campaign. The money would be used—"

I said, "This isn't Kentucky. I'm an independent, having no special love for Republicans. I haven't given any politician a nickel—not in 2010, not in 2012, and not this year. Sorry, you wasted a trip."

He sighed. "I don't want to mention this, I don't. But this week, I will be proposing a bill to outlaw multiple-partner cohabitation. Such a bill polls well with family-values voters, but it would be hard on Mr. Hefner and on you, I think."

"What are we talking here? One guy shacks up with more than one girl, and *boom*, they all go to prison?"

"Exactly."

I laughed. "You cocksucker, you're lying to me. The reddest of Red States is Utah, and that place is crawling with polygamists. If your bill were to pass, every Republican in Utah would hate your guts, even the guys with only one wife. Which means, forget about you becoming president."

Senator "Happy Larry" still had the big smile. "I'm not kidding about the bill. I intend to propose it this week."

"Why would I give you a million dollars if then Anna Kay, my *haremées*, and I all got sent to prison?"

"But if you gave me a million-dollar donation, I'd kill the bill. There is no value in my worrying a major political donor."

"Ah, so those are my choices? Give you a million-dollar donation, otherwise I risk everyone here in the mansion going to prison?"

"Marvin, what you're doing with these girls, it's *immoral*."

"But for a million bucks, you'd overlook that?"

He shrugged.

I said, "Well, there is 'immoral' and there is *immoral*. Take misappropriation—*that* is immoral, don't you agree?"

Senator Larry gave me a puzzled look.

I picked up my desk phone and speed-dialed Fatima. "Fatima, would you send SJ-1 in now, please? Code One."

Not one second later, the computer-room door opened and Fatima's silver sex-slave walked in. SJ-1 was carrying a green-plastic laptop computer.

A unique green-plastic laptop computer.

But the senator's attention clearly wasn't on the computer. He said, "Who is this? Or maybe I should say, *What* is this? And Marvin, we agreed that nobody but you and me would be in this room."

"No, I said I wouldn't bring Anna Kay in, or Fatima. I didn't say Word One about SJ-1. Senator, this is SJ-1, my housekeeper's assistant and sex-slave. She—"

"Good grief, you *are* a decadent bunch, aren't you?"

"Anyway, senator, SJ-1 has found something interesting about misappropriation. *Yours*."

SJ-1 had grabbed a TV tray and had set it in front of the couch. Now she set the laptop on the tray. She didn't plug the laptop into a wall socket, because she didn't need to.

After several seconds of SJ-1 typing on the keyboard and working the trackball, she said in a calm voice, "This is a bank account in the First Bank of the Bahamas. It has $4,231,865.88 in it, as you see here. The name on the account—"

"Good god, my chief of staff has a Bahamas bank account?"

"Incorrect," SJ-1 said calmly. Calmly she added, "The name on the account is that of your chief of staff. But the email address attached to this account is BobCLawrence at Hotmail-dot-com. Bob Lawrence was your brother, who died in an auto accident in 1977. The password attached to this account was 'Fluffypuff,' which is the name of your wife Jenny's poodle."

Lawrence said, "What do you mean, the password *was* 'Fluffypuff'?"

"This unit changed the password forty-seven hours ago. The password now is 675_sTyuBCvP$_z6—plus 110 more characters, but they're boring."

I said, "Tell Senator Lawrence about the emails, SJ-1."

Calmly she replied, "Everything this unit has just told you has been written up as emails, with attached PNG-file screenshots of this bank-account information. These emails have been sent to TV stations and newspapers in Lexington-Fayette and in Louisville."

"Tell him when you sent those emails, SJ-1," I said.

"Just before this unit walked through that door," she calmly replied.

I said, "You shouldn't have tried to extort me for a million bucks, senator. *Very* uncool."

Happy Larry wasn't smiling now; his face was furious. "Whatever your game is, I'll deny everything! You can't prove a thing!"

"Actually, I can." I picked up the desk phone, and asked Fatima to send in "the camera crew."

In walked a reporter and cameraman from Channel Ten, along with Gennifer Ashton. Gennifer was my publicist (and former *haremée*), but she used to work for Channel Ten. And at the same moment that the TV people walked in—

Anna Kay stood up from behind my computer desk, shut off the cassette recorder she was holding, ejected the cassette tape, and handed the tape to Gennifer.

Gennifer passed the tape to the aggressive Channel Ten woman who was holding the microphone.

I looked at Senator Lawrence, who was trying to no-comment the TV reporter. I said, "Senator, the reason I never argued to bring my wife into this room during our meeting was that she was already here."

He said sadly, "The taped conversation will hurt me. Those emails will *kill* me."

I shrugged. "What can I say? SJ-1 has a real talent for finding information on a computer. *Any* computer."

SJ-1 did indeed have talent as a hacker. Paula Sarin had been fortunate to find Sheila Johansson. But part of SJ-1's success was due to her GT Technologies laptop computer.

The *GT*, it turned out, stood for *Green Tribe*.

I was pleased with myself. I had hurt a dishonest politician in a way that he could neither fight nor brush off, and there was nothing clearly impossible (meaning, magical) about what I had done.

****

Wednesday noon, October 22, 2014

Vinnie watched Senator Lawrence get arrested. Happy Larry's arrest was shown live on CNN. Vinnie was so angry, he wanted to shoot Happy Larry in the head, also live on CNN. Lawrence could have become president, and Vinnie could have become the president's puppeteer, except that Happy Larry, that *idiot*, had to act greedy!

Vinnie was so pissed at Happy Larry, Vinnie went to Senator Lawrence's house and magically seduced his trophy wife Jenny and his maid Beulah. But even the threesome that Vinnie got into, didn't soothe his anger much.

But the focus of Vinnie's anger switched completely when Kharmesh informed him that Marvin Harper—who had caused Senator Lawrence to get arrested, and so had ruined Vinnie's great plan—was the master of Fatima, the green-eyed genie bitch who had so disrespected Vinnie.

Vinnie vowed: Marvin Harper would somehow pay, and so would Fatima. *Count on it.*

Chapter 24
We're Off To West Virginia

The Monday after Almira and Elvira were paroled, they started their work at my Harper Foundation. Their work was entry-level.

The Foundation subscribes to newspapers from every place in the USA that prints a newspaper. Want to know what's happening in Muleshoe, Texas or in Picayune, Mississippi? The Harper Foundation has the latest news from those places (making allowance for mail-delivery times).

The twins' job was to go through each day's newspapers and cut out any news article where someone was in a jam—somebody's house burned down, or someone died in an accident and left a wife and children behind, and so on.

It was necessary work, what the twins were doing, but it didn't feel like "charity." The Harper Foundation's newspaper-clippers would never meet the people they helped.

That all changed three months after Almira and Elvira started working for me.

****

Thursday morning, October 23, 2014

"... explosion and tunnel collapse at the Number 3 Mine in Unionville, West Virginia," the news anchor informed me. "Twenty-one miners are dead, injured, or missing. The cause of the accident is not known at this time. The Red Cross has responded with a Disaster Action Team and has dispatched two Emergency Response Vehicles. The Red Cross is requesting donations of . . ."

The time was morning. I had just gotten out of the shower and was getting dressed in my bedroom. I had the bedroom TV on, tuned to MS-NBC. I was barely paying attention; the news anchor's voice was background noise at first.

Now I listened closely to the news about the mine disaster, because I was in a position to help the Red Cross. Everything they were asking for, except for blood donations, I could make happen simply by flashing my credit card.

The only trouble was, helping people by credit card seemed lazy to me.

Broadcast with the anchorman's talk was video: a helicopter view of what looked like a treeless mountain with a square hole dug in its side; railroad tracks lead in and out of that square hole. On top of the treeless hill were three giant fans; black-smoke flames were shooting up through one of those fans.

Even someone mining-ignorant like me could figure out that this wasn't supposed to happen.

The blades of the enflamed fan weren't turning, I noticed; I didn't know if this was normal or not.

By the time I'd walked downstairs to the monster kitchen, I'd decided what to do about the mine disaster.

Many young women sat at tables in the monster kitchen, eating breakfast. Among them was Virgilia O'Keefe—Mensa member; a former sex-slave of my Uncle Warren and later, of me; ex-stripper; a former genie-master of Fatima (for three minutes); April 2012 *Playboy* centerfold; and now the CEO of the Harper Foundation.

Rather than take my usual seat, I walked into the middle of the kitchen. The women eating (Anna Kay, Virgilia, both twins, and many others) and the women cooking (Fatima and five others) all gave me their undivided attention—

I said, "There's been a mine disaster in West Virginia. I'm loading up the airplane with everything that I can stuff into it, and I'll be flying down there. Anna Kay, will you come?"

"Of course I will," she said, smiling.

"Everyone who works at the Foundation, from Virgilia on down, I want you to continue what you're doing. Now, in addition to myself and Anna Kay, I'm going to want two young women to help me. Anyone volunteer?"

Every last one of the *haremées* raised her hand; many raised both hands.

With one exception: Elvira slumped down in her chair.

What a surprise.

****

After breakfast, I took my wife, Fatima, and *haremées* Heloise and Jodie to Sam's Club, and we bought the place out. Baby formula, canned chicken, boys' and girls' clothing—I bought everything nonperishable that a miner's wife or child might need.

We were in the Sam's Club parking lot, loading up our purchases into my tour bus, when my smartphone rang. Calling was Aunt Claire.

She told me that "Lois" (my mother) had told her about my plans for West Virginia. Aunt Claire asked who was going.

I replied, "Besides me? Anna Kay and two young women from the harem, who are there basically to hand out stuff, smile, and look sympathetic."

Aunt Claire asked, "Have you picked the two women yet?"

"Nope. Got lots of volunteers, though."

"Would you please take Almira and Elvira? I think the trip would do them good."

I tried a dodge: "Aunt Claire, they're ex-cons. They can't leave this city without permission." I don't add what I was really thinking: *Take Elvira with me? No way.*

Aunt Claire said, "Then would you please talk to whoever needs to be talked to? I really think it would be good for the twins to see you helping people."

I felt a moment's annoyance.

Then I remembered the only other time that Aunt Claire had made a request of me: to visit my sick Uncle Warren in the hospital. Aunt Claire had requested this for an unselfish reason: because Uncle Warren needed a visit from family.

I had big misgivings, but I respected Aunt Claire's judgment. So I replied, "I'll ask their parole officer, but I won't argue with him if he says no."

****

I forgot that Parole Officer Martin Howard was a let's-just-be-friends semi-slave of mine. When I asked about taking the twins to West Virginia, he immediately said yes.

****

Just before three young women and I drove away from the mansion, Fatima took me aside. "I'm surprised you didn't ask me to make the trip with you."

I replied, "Why? Coal-mining country is ugly, Fatima."

"Why take me? So if something bad happens, I'd be there to protect you."

I put my big hands on Fatima's shoulders. "I'll be handing out food and water, and talking to reporters. No way will I be in danger. Stay in this city, Fatima, and wait for my call."

Then I added, "Please remind Gennifer to put out a press release before my airplane arrives in West Virginia."

Chapter 25
Vinnie Gets A Phone Call

While Vinnie was driving along the highway, his smartphone rang.

Vinnie's phone didn't know the phone number, but Vinnie recognized that it was a Louisville, Kentucky area code.

Vinnie was surprised. After Senator Lawrence's arrest and the collapse of his re-election campaign, Vinnie had not expected any more phone calls from Louisville.

Vinnie said cautiously, "Hello?"

"Hello, Mr. Vega, I'm John Chandler Snow, CEO of Collier International. I'm told you can help me with a problem I have."

"How did you get my number?"

"Collier International is based out of Louisville, and so I'm *very* close friends with Happy Larry. His campaign manager gave me your number when I asked."

"I'm busy right now," Vinnie said. Which was true—he was driving back to Boston with Kharmesh, with plans to resume personal control of his supergang. "Why are you calling me?"

"Because I have a business proposition for Vinnie Lavagetto, the gangster, whom I understand you know *well*."

Vinnie was shocked silent. At last he said, "You think I know this Vinnie Lavagetto guy? A gangster?"

Snow laughed. "Not just *any* gangster. You've built up quite an empire, Lavagetto, and I respect that."

"Who else knows this about me?"

"Happy Larry, for one. But he didn't give a rat's ass, so long as you were useful to him. Anyway, I want to hire you for a project."

"I'm listening."

"Collier International owns coal mines, including the mine in Unionville, West Virginia—the mine that's in the news right now."

"I don't follow news much, unless it's about me."

"Here's the short version: The mine is messed up. No coal is getting mined while all the miners are being brought out, dead or alive. Then the mine stays closed *and unproductive* while the government investigates what causes the accident. Anyway, if the MSHA—"

"The what?"

"The Mine Safety and Health Administration, the government agency that is in charge of coal mines. Anyway, if they decide that the Number 3 mine is *seriously* fucked up, they can close the mine for good. If that happens, Collier International is out all the money we've spent."

"So where do I come in?"

"It's possible that Collier International was negligent in how we ran that mine. Not saying we *were*, just saying it's possible. Anyway, coal miners are all complainers and socialists, and I guarantee that they want to trash-talk CI to the investigators. I don't want that to happen."

"Or I could skip the miners. Send some fellas to talk to the government types. Persuade 'em to write a friendly report."

"*No.* Then the FBI gets called in—that's the *last* thing I want. Confine your persuasion to the miners only."

"Fine, whatever," Vinnie said.

Vinnie and Snow negotiated price and payment terms. Snow insisted that whatever goons that Vinnie wound up using, came from outside of both Kentucky and West Virginia, so that their faces wouldn't be known to local law-enforcement officers. Vinnie agreed to that.

Eventually Vinnie asked, "Is that it? That everything?"

Snow replied, "One more thing. You've heard of Marvin Harper, the 'hero billionaire'? He's the man who Happy Larry tried to shake down for a million dollars."

To which Vinnie mentally added, *And who I got a score to settle with.* Aloud, Vinnie said, "What about him?"

"Marvin Harper's just announced he's flying to Unionville. To help all those poor, hurt coal miners."

"Yeah? Then I will make *goddamn* sure my boys rearrange his face. I had a sweet deal going with Happy Larry, and Harper messed it up."

"*No.* In fact, *double no.* Remember that Harper's called 'Batman' by the news media. If your boys get near him, *he* might rearrange *their* faces. Plus, he's not only got fists, but he's got lawyers. Reporters hang on his every word. So stay away from him."

"We'll see," Vinnie replied. "I owe Harper big payback, and I'm not gonna forget that."

****

Vinnie talked things over with Kharmesh. Kharmesh not only was willing to help, he even made some suggestions.

That do-gooder Marvin Harper and his bitch genie Fatima were going *down.*

Chapter 26
Sidelined In Unionville

Unionville, West Virginia—population: four thousand—didn't have an airport. So I flew my airplane to the nearby city of Fairmont, landed there, and then rented a truck.

"Marvin, why do *we* have to unload the airplane? Why do *we* have to load up the truck? You're rich, go hire some locals." Thus complained Elvira soon after we landed.

Even though I was doing most of the lifting and carrying. *Sigh.*

Once we four people got into the truck, we hit up Fairmont's grocery stores, buying perishable food. In the Wal-Mart in Fairmont, I overheard Elvira say to her sister, "These people talk funny." I hoped that I wasn't going to regret bringing Elvira on this trip.

****

We stopped at the Unionville Inn, and I paid for four guests in a room with two double beds. Once we'd unloaded our luggage, I drove the rental truck to the coal mine.

It turned out that for mine-rescue, the miners used well-trained teams, which I clearly didn't qualify for, despite my muscles. Also, I was told, my 6'8" height was actually a disadvantage in the mine. Bottom line: I wasn't included in any rescue teams after we arrived in town.

That was embarrassing, but I shrugged it off. After all, the trapped miners and their families had much worse problems to deal with than public embarrassment like I had.

By the time we arrived at the mine, the casualty figures had changed. Two miners (Mickey and Jim) had made it to a rescue chamber, which was gastight and which had food, water, and a two-way radio; so they were all right, though still stuck in the mine. One miner had walked out of the mine. The bodies of two dead miners had been recovered.

That left seventeen miners out of twenty-two with their status unknown, and potentially nineteen miners dead.

For the moment, rescue attempts were stymied. One mineshaft had collapsed due to explosion, and that shaft also had too much methane gas in it. By an unfortunate coincidence, the exhaust fan that would normally remove the methane from that shaft was the same exhaust fan that had been flamed in the mine explosion.

Meanwhile, the rescuers were working on reopening the blocked mineshaft, and then jury-rigging a methane-exhaust setup. I again offered to help with clearing the mineshaft; again I was politely turned down.

Needless to say, the crowd behind the police barricade was jittery. Nobody was happy and relaxed, not even members of a family whose miner was safe.

I decided that if I wasn't allowed to lift fallen rocks, I'd do what I could—

Mike Hawthorne, the president of the United Mine Workers local chapter, gave me a list of all the trapped miners and the names of their wives and children. When I had the list, I opened up the back of the rental truck and started giving away food and clothing to family members of the miners. It didn't matter if the miner in question was "status unknown," had already escaped, or had made it to the rescue chamber, his family got free stuff from me.

****

Giving out the booty didn't take long. So when the truck was empty, nothing had changed with the mine and miners—

• a mineshaft was collapsed in one place, blocking rescue;

• that mineshaft needed to be vented of methane; and

• seventeen miners still were not accounted for.

Five hours later, we on the surface got the word: the rescuers had entered the mineshaft.

Ten minutes after that, the rescuers brought up the third dead body.

One of the rescuers walked out of the mine carrying a five-gallon pump-sprayer that was burned and dented. I didn't know what to make of that.

I asked Mike Hawthorne about the pump sprayer. He told me, "We're supposed to have a sprinkler system that wets down the walls. You know, to hold down the coal dust? But the sprinkler system was busted for part of that shaft, and CI"—Collier International—"was taking their sweet-ass time about fixing the sprinklers. So guys were coming to work with pump sprayers and wetting down the walls thesselves. Of course, every second a man is spraying the walls is a second he ain't making quota."

Meanwhile, the man who was carrying the burned pump-sprayer was walking toward a man who was standing outside with a clipboard and an MSHA windbreaker. But before the man carrying the pump-sprayer got there, a man in a suit hurried up to that man and started yelling at him.

At which point, the man with the pump-sprayer yelled back. The two men argued for a bit, then the rescuer walked around Suit Man and walked up to the MSHA official. Suit Man yelled something at the rescuer's retreating back that sounded threatening.

"Stupid CI shithead," Mike Hawthorne muttered. He walked up to Suit Man, spoke briefly, then Mike walked over and talked to the rescuer and the MSHA official.

****

For the twins, Anna Kay, and me, all there was to do now was to stand in front of the mine, along with the trapped miners' families and friends, and wait.

"There are three assholes who keep staring at us," Almira said in a low voice.

Elvira added, "Dressed big-city, and looking at us *way* too much."

"Yeah, I noticed them," I quietly replied.

In the crowd, there were three men who didn't spend any time looking at the entrance to the mine, but they kept looking in our direction. Those three men all had new clothes (few of the miners' family members did), and two of the three men had pompadour haircuts.

I decided that they were looking our way because they were thinking unhealthy thoughts about my women—all three of whom, recall Reader, were big-breasted hotties. But I decided that those guys wouldn't dare pull any shit with me standing nearby.

****

It was night outside when the rescuers came out of the mine with Mickey and Jim (the two men from the rescue chamber), along with the nineteenth dead body.

The two living miners were cheered by the crowd. The police didn't object when their wives pushed the barricades aside and ran to their husbands, with children running up behind their mothers.

But before and after this moment, the crowd was somber, and I knew why.

Not only did nineteen families have to deal with the stark human grief of losing their husband/father, but these families now had to pay for a funeral.

And just from looking at these people manning the barricades—how worn their clothing was, and how old were the cars and trucks they drove—I knew that none of them could afford a funeral. Not without sacrifice.

Mike Hawthorne was holding a battery-powered bullhorn, though he hadn't used it much. I tapped him on the arm and pointed at the bullhorn. He handed it to me.

I stepped around the police barricade, took three steps more, turned to the crowd, and turned on the bullhorn—

"FAMILIES OF THE DEAD MINERS, I AM MARVIN HARPER THE BILLIONAIRE. I AM SORRY FOR YOUR LOSSES. I CANNOT IMAGINE YOUR PAIN AND YOUR WORRIES RIGHT NOW, BUT YOU DON'T NEED TO WORRY ABOUT PAYING FOR YOUR LOVED ONE'S FUNERAL. GIVE YOUR MAN THE FUNERAL HE DESERVES, AND I WILL PAY FOR IT."

When I handed the bullhorn back to Mike Hawthorne, he murmured, "Part of our union dues goes to pay for funerals. I'm not complaining, but you don't need to do this."

I murmured back, "You might need to use that money for lawyers instead."

Mike slapped me on the back. "Marvin, you're good people. There's a bar on Route 250 called The Seam, where us miners go to relax. If you come tonight, I'll buy you a beer and introduce you around to the men."

****

Just before the twins, Anna Kay, and I all climbed into the rental truck, I looked at the twins. "Almira and Elvira, you helped out a lot today. Thank you."

Almira beamed. Elvira looked confused. I guess Elvira didn't hear sincere compliments often.

Then the four of us got into the rental truck. I drove us back to the Unionville Inn, parked the truck, and we walked back to our motel room. I told the women not to open the door for anyone but me, then I walked out of the room.

I walked into town, heading straight for Abernathy and Mazzare Funeral Home.

I was planning to walk into the funeral home, tell the undertaker, "Put the nineteen funerals on my credit card," sign some forms, and walk out. I expected the visit to the funeral home to be no more exciting than ordering a hamburger at McDonald's.

Reader, it's a good thing I'm a billionaire, because I'd starve as a fortuneteller.

Chapter 27
Summit Conference 2

Thursday, October 23, 2014, 8:23 p.m. local time
At a picnic table in Joe Henry Park
Yuma, Arizona, USA

"You *know* Green Tribe and Pink Tribe would have made you surrender," Ashnadim said to Hakeezib.

"No, the Blue Tribe would have hurt both your tribes till *you* surrendered," Hakeezib replied.

"How lucky for you," Sigvard said to Hakeezib, "that you will never be proven wrong. Since there will never ever be a Djinn War."

"Luck has nothing to do with it," Hakeezib replied. "I know one of you summoned the human king, Solomon. I haven't figured out which of you did it—"

Sigvard laughed contemptuously. "The only thing I would summon a human for, is to clean camel dung off my boots. Or elk dung, but those days are long gone. Ah, the seasons change, and even the positions of the stars change, but Blue Tribe refusing to face facts goes on forever."

Ashnadim said, "Let's change the subject. *One* human we all can speak well of, Marvin Harper of the Six Wishes—"

As Sigvard nodded, Hakeezib said, "*I* don't speak well of him. He's just another magicless, walking dustball."

Ashnadim said, "Correction: He is a *kind and generous* magicless, walking dustball. He is in Unionville, West Virginia, here in the United States, helping human strangers who are trapped in a coal mine."

Ashnadim was an ally; so Sigvard didn't mention that the humans mined coal because they could not magically create fire; and *these* humans were trapped because they could not *foom* themselves out of the mine, as a *djinni* could.

Meanwhile, Hakeezib was saying, "Marvin Harper is in Unionville? Why does that place sound familiar?"

Hakeezib clasped his hands together on the picnic table, and stared straight ahead—or so he appeared. Sigvard knew that Hakeezib probably was working his scrying ball at the moment; and was covering up this activity with illusion, in order to fool any humans watching.

That illusion fooled the eyes of *djinn* too—but unlike humans, a *djinni* could cast a spell to pierce the illusion, if he suspected the illusion's presence. But Sigvard was feeling lazy at the moment; he didn't bother.

After 10.6 seconds of Hakeezib seeming to be motionless, his face turned toward Ashnadim. "Kharmesh and his master, Vinnie Lavagetto, also are in Unionville. But bound *djinni* Fatima of the Green Tribe *is not* in Unionville, and in fact *is forbidden* to go there."

Hakeezib's smile was cruel. "I have no idea what is going on, but I'm sure it will be entertaining to watch. Especially since it seems that Marvin Harper doesn't know about Vinnie Lavagetto and Kharmesh being nearby."

Chapter 28
Elvira's World Changes

Unionville Inn, Room 111

"What are you doing?" Almira demanded to know.

Elvira was standing by the closed motel-room door. One hand was on the doorknob; her other hand was holding an empty plastic ice bucket. "I'm going to get ice. Duh, twin."

"Marvin wants us to stay in the room till he gets back," Anna Kay said.

Elvira rolled her eyes. "There isn't a fridge in this room, and the bottles of pop all are warm."

Almira said, "Marvin told us to stay inside, so I'm staying inside. End of story."

Elvira rolled her eyes again. "R-i-ght, because you always do what Marvin tells you to."

"Actually, I do," Almira replied, "because making Marvin happy makes *me* happy."

Elvira said, "Walking to the ice machine and back takes what, five minutes? I'm willing to risk my rape and gruesome murder to get my Coke cold."

Almira sighed. "Shit, twin, why do you always fight Marvin, when he deserves to be served?"

Elvira tensed; Almira might order her to stay inside, and Elvira would do it.

But then Almira gestured Elvira out the door. "Go. I don't like warm Coke either."

Anna Kay walked to the door. "Yes, go, Elvira, if you insist so much. But I'm locking the door behind you. Knock when you get back."

Sure enough, Elvira hadn't taken two steps out the door when she heard the door lock behind her.

****

Merry Mountaineers Motel, Room 262
Unionville, West Virginia

Young American men in 2014, even gangsters, have smartphones. Redheaded Sean Callahan was in his motel room, watching TV, when his phone rang.

The caller was the Big Boss, Vinnie Lavagetto.

Mr. Lavagetto didn't waste time on chit-chat: "Brandon and Big Pete are with you, right?"

"Uh, right. You need something, Mr. Lavagetto?"

"You three go to the Unionville Inn. It's on the other side of town—"

Which didn't mean a lot, Sean knew. Unionville was the size of a postage stamp, compared to Boston.

"—and find the downstairs ice machine. There's a girl there, she's got dark-brown hair, blue eyes, big tits, and an ice bucket. I need for you to grab her before she goes back into her room."

"Um, okay," Sean replied. "Who is she? Does she have bodyguards?"

"She and two other women came with Marvin Harper. But he's nowhere near the motel. Now shut up and *move*."

Sean shut up; and then he, Brandon, and Big Pete *moved*.

****

Elvira was waiting at the ice machine. At the moment, a beautiful blonde in her thirties was filling her own ice bucket.

The blond shut the ice machine's lid, then turned to walk past Elvira. She glanced at Elvira's face, then exclaimed, "Oh, I know you!"

"Huh? How do you know my name?"

The blonde had a practiced smile. "I don't know your name, dear, but I want to. You're with Marvin Harper, right? You and your twin?"

Elvira wondered, *Is this woman hitting on me?* Aloud, she said, "Yes, my sister and I are with Marvin Harper and his wife. We're trying to help the miners."

The blonde smiled again. "That's why *I'm* here. I'm Eleanor Buford, of the Richmond, Virginia Bufords, but right now I'm here with the Red Cross." Eleanor put out her hand to shake.

"I'm Elvira LeClerc. My sister is named Almira." Elvira shook Eleanor's hand.

Eleanor smiled. "If Marvin were here, I'd thank him on behalf of the Red Cross for what's he's done here. But since he's not here and you are, I'll thank *you*. Elvira, America needs more kind-hearted people like you and your sister who help neighbors in need."

Elvira was stunned. She and Almira had been called many things in twenty-six years, but never *kind-hearted.*

Elvira said, "Well, uh, that's nice of you to say, but Almie and I, we're not really—"

"Oh, dear. Was I wrong? Is this your job?"

"No, Marvin asked us to come here, and so here we are. But it's not like Almie and I are *saints.*"

Eleanor laughed. "Dear, I'm no saint either! But it does you credit that you're helping these poor miners *and* you're acting modest."

With that, Eleanor gave Elvira another socialite smile, touched her arm, and walked away with her ice bucket.

Elvira thought, *Wow, someone actually admires me?*

The ice machine was next to a hallway, which led to a door marked "Laundry Room." As Elvira was filling her ice bucket, a woman walked out of the laundry room, looked around, saw Elvira, and walked toward her. Up close, Elvira saw that the woman was wearing a nametag that said, "Unionville Inn—Hazelle McCarthy."

Hazelle said, "Um, pardon me, ma'am, but you're with Marvin Harper, the hero millionaire?"

"Actually, he's a billionaire," Elvira replied.

"Oh wow," Hazelle breathed. Then she squared her shoulders and said, "You folks came all the way here to Unionville to help people out. That's a mighty fine thing you're doing."

"Well, we didn't actually do that much. Marvin bought food and clothing, and today we gave them away."

Hazelle shook her head. "Ma'am, y'all done a lot! My cousin Joanna took charity from you folks today. She had to, Mark died today. Anyway, Joanna was afeared that she'd be asked lots of rude questions by y'all. But the only thing the woman said to her was, 'Your name is on the list. How can I help you?' Maybe *you* were the woman who helped Joanna?"

Elvira shook her head. "There were three women in that truck. It was probably someone else."

Hazelle said, "Listen, I need to get back to the office; we're hopping tonight. But I just want to say, ma'am, you're a good woman for coming with Marvin Harper and helping out strangers. For Joanna and her kids, thank you very much."

Elvira was trying not to cry. "You're welcome, Hazelle. I'm glad we could help Joanna and her kids, and I'm sorry about their loss."

Hazelle said, "You folks have a good evening now, y'hear?" Then she hurried away.

Now Elvira became aware of running footsteps. Three men were running toward her, the redhead in the group holding a smartphone to his ear.

After the men stopped in front of her, Smartphone Man asked, "Are you Elvira, one of the twins who's here with Marvin Harper?"

Elvira stood proud and straight. "Yes, I am."

The biggest man stepped up close to Elvira, and she was shocked to feel the pain of a knifepoint pricking her skin.

Smartphone Man said, "Us four are gonna take a nice walk to Room 111. Then girlie, you're gonna get us inside."

Chapter 29
At the Funeral Home

Ten minutes after I walked out of our motel, I walked into Abernathy and Mazzare Funeral Home. Naturally, since it was long after normal business hours, there was nobody in the reception area.

I couldn't imagine what it must be like to be the only mortuary in town, and to have nineteen people die at once. I'm sure the stress was killing them (pardon the expression).

Nobody was there to stop me from slipping through double doors that took me into a terra-cotta-tiled hallway. I heard voices, and I headed that direction.

". . .ain't asking you, the big boss is *telling* you: The money you make from this big bunch of funerals, you share with *us*. Got it?" The speaker had a Massachusetts accent.

A tenor voice said, "But we can't afford to pay you protection. We're just a little-town funeral home, we're not raking it in!"

Massachusetts replied, "Yeah? Right now you got stiffs out the wazoo, and that do-gooder rich guy is gonna pay you to plant 'em all fancy."

A baritone voice said, "So you think we're going to be rich after this? Maybe where *you* come from, funerals are gold caskets and Italian-marble headstones, but people here won't go for that. Even with Marvin Harper paying the bill."

Massachusetts said, "Boo-hoo, breaking my heart. You got a choice. You gimme a thousand bucks cash right now, or Mr. Lavagetto—"

I thought, *As in "Vinnie Lavagetto"? Nah, he must mean a different guy.*

"—is gonna send some boys to trash your place, and some other undertaker guys will get to plant those dead guys."

I'd heard enough. I walked through double doors into a workroom, and saw one of the pompadour men who'd been staring at us earlier. Now he was five feet in front of me, facing left, holding a gun on two other men.

Loudly I said, "The do-gooder rich guy says you're a scumbag."

Pompadour whirled around and pointed his gun at me.

Jeez, not this again.

I'd entered the workroom by a stainless-steel table, on which lay the naked corpse of an old woman. By the corpse's head was a rolling table with cosmetics, hairbrushes, and a big pair of shears on it.

I grabbed a hairbrush and threw it at Pompadour's eyes.

He put up both hands in an instinctive move to protect his face.

I dived down onto the floor in front of him, tucked my head, and rolled into a half-somersault. My feet came out of the half-somersault to hit Pompadour in the chest. *Slap!*

Whump! Pompadour got knocked back against a polished wooden coffin on a gurney. He gasped on impact.

It took only a second for me to go from having my ass, back, and head lying on the floor, to standing on two feet. That was when I saw that Pompadour was not holding his gun in his hand anymore.

Score one for the do-gooder rich guy.

Less than one second later, I had Pompadour spun around, and I had his arm pulled up behind his back. Pompadour grunted from the pain.

I looked over at the undertakers, who both were staring at me openmouthed. I calmly asked, "You got any duct tape?"

They did. But it turned out that I couldn't effectively tape Pompadour's hands together, because he was wearing a long-sleeved shirt and a long-sleeved jacket.

Then I remembered seeing the big shears on the rolling table. I told the undertakers, "Cut his sleeves off."

A minute later, Pompadour's hands were taped behind his back, and Mr. Abernathy (the baritone) and Mr. Mazzare (the tenor) both were looking relaxed. Pompadour was *not* looking relaxed, and was talking trash to all three of us.

I said, "When you talk to Mr. Lavagetto, you tell him that these two men are under my protection."

Pompadour said, "I'm not saying shit about you!"

"Then you're not going to have an excuse why you didn't come back with a thousand bucks. Mr. Lavagetto will be *so disappointed* in you. That could be painful."

"Nah, I'll just tell him that I was a soft touch today. Then tomorrow I'll come back with more guys. And I'll demand two thousand. Or three thousand."

Pompadour glared at the undertakers. *"And you better have it when I ask for it!"*

Mazzare gulped. "Maybe we better pay him *now*."

"Damned straight," Pompadour replied.

"But we don't have a thousand dollars we can spare, much less *three* thousand," Abernathy said to Mazzare.

"Not my problem," Pompadour said, laughing.

I decided to have some fun with this guy. I laughed *louder* than he was laughing, which quickly shut him up.

I said, "You dummy. You've just given these men reason to kill you."

"Yeah, but they're pussies."

My smile was evil. "They have a cremation oven here."

Pompadour's face lost its smile.

I continued, "They can burn you up, put your ashes in a coffin, bury the coffin, and there'd be no proof you were ever here. Looky, here's an available coffin." I nodded toward the coffin that Pompadour had been knocked into.

"Bullshit," Pompadour said. "You're trying to fuck with my head."

Mazzare said, "Not *this* coffin, because it'll be open during Mrs. Undersee's viewing." He gestured toward the corpse.

Abernathy said thoughtfully, "But Mr. Mailey gets buried tomorrow. We add the ashes to his coffin after his viewing is over, and before we put his coffin in the hearse. An hour later, this man's ashes are six feet under. By sundown, the hole is filled in."

Abernathy looked at Mazzare. Mazzare looked at Abernathy. Then they both looked at Pompadour. Who gulped, then whimpered.

Mazzare said, "No need to waste a coffin for the cremation. We could use a cardboard shipping box. Who'll notice one less shipping box in the Dumpster?"

The smirking and laughing Pompadour of a minute ago was long gone. Now the front of his pants had a big wet spot. Not to mention—

"Jeez," I said, "he's shit his pants!"

Abernathy shrugged. "We're used to it."

Then Abernathy looked at me and said, "If you'll hold his feet while I tape his legs together, we can handle the rest."

That's when I realized that my joke was about to get out of hand.

I said, "Change of plans, gentlemen. Get those shears and cut his clothes off. *All* his clothes off."

＊＊＊＊

Two minutes later, Pompadour was wearing nothing but shoes (and duct tape, around his wrists). I had his shit-smelling wallet in my pocket.

I said to him, "You've lost your gun. It's theirs now."

Mazzare said, "I don't want his gun. Did he bring any calzone?"

My final words to Abernathy and Mazzare were, "I'll be in tomorrow to talk about paying for the funerals."

Then I added an aside to Pompadour, "Not *yours,* so relax."

I put my hand between Pompadour's shoulder blades and pushed him forward. "Now you and I are walking out of here, then we're going to walk along Route 250 till we get to a bar called The Seam."

"We're *walking?* Walking *outside?* I'm fucking naked!"

"Uh-huh. Remember how you said that no way would Mr. Lavagetto find out that the funeral home is under my protection? Well, I want to make sure he gets that word, even if you don't tell him."

****

As I was frog-marching Pompadour toward the bar that Mike Hawthorne had told me about, I thought of calling Anna Kay. But I decided not to—I needed my right hand to keep Pompadour walking on the correct path, and I'm not skilled at working a smartphone with only my left hand.

Chapter 30
My Enemy Is Active

I had intended for what happened to Pompadour to be a joke, although a cruel one. I had planned to frog-march him to the bar, walk him inside, announce who he was and what he had done, and give him his wallet back, plus change from my pocket. He would use the pay phone—every bar has a pay phone, right?—to call his gangster friends in town, they would pick him up, and Mike Hawthorne and I would jeer at the gangsters when they showed up. After that, I would drink beers with Mike, and he would introduce me to other miners.

That was the plan. But the plan went screwy.

Reader, the last time there was such a gap between what I intended to do and what actually happened was when I polished up an old brass lamp so I could sell it on eBay.

But this time, the "what actually happened" events were not fun to live through.

****

I pushed Pompadour into The Seam. I looked around for Mike Hawthorne, president of the local chapter of United Mine Workers, but did not see him.

He had told me he would be here, so I figured he was in the restroom at the moment.

Meanwhile, everybody in The Seam was staring at us. I am used to it now; but recall, Reader, that Pompadour was getting stared at because he was *naked*.

I took Pompadour's wallet out of my pants pocket and put the wallet in his left hand. I dug a bunch of coins out of another pocket and put the coins in his right hand. Then I said to the room, "This guy was just at the funeral home, where I caught him trying to shake down the undertakers for a thousand dollars. I brought him here so he can call his gangster friends and arrange a ride."

I smiled and added, "Also, so he can ask them to bring him some clothes."

A half-dozen men stood up then. Like Mike Hawthorne, their faces and hands looked dirty even after they'd washed them. The six men came over to Pompadour and me, and their faces were *furious.*

One man said, "He's a gangster?"

I replied, "Yes, he—"

Pompadour still was holding his wallet in his left hand (because he had no other way to carry it). One of the miners grabbed the wallet out of Pompadour's hand, opened the wallet, yanked the cash out, handed the cash to another miner, and threw the wallet on the floor.

The wallet-thief miner said, "This money will go toward Mickey's and Jim's hospital bills."

I was confused. "Mickey and Jim are in the hospital? A few hours ago, they were fine." They'd spent all of the hours before rescue in the rescue chamber, after all.

Now another miner quit glaring at Pompadour long enough to say to me, "*They* aren't in the hospital, their *wives* are. Gangsters forced their way into both their houses tonight, and beat up their wives. Jim and Mickey got told that when the gubbermint guys talked to them, they were to say only nice things about CI and Mine Number 3. *Or else.*"

I was still processing this when the wallet-thief miner grabbed Pompadour's right arm; another miner quickly grabbed Pompadour's left arm. Wallet-Thief Miner said to Pompadour, "Poor man, you're probably lost, being from out of town and all. We'll make sure you get back to your *friends.*"

A miner who'd been quiet up till now said, "Yeah, gangster, we're gonna *take you for a ride*. You don't need to thank us."

With that, the six miners dragged Pompadour out of The Seam. His de-cashed wallet still was laying on the floor.

****

I tried talking to the remaining miners in the bar, but I didn't make headway. I did not know any of them except Mike Hawthorne, whom I had counted on to introduce me around.

The miners were not rude or hateful. But between the deaths of nineteen of their friends and coworkers, and Mickey and Jim being harassed by gangsters, the miners were not friendly, either. Nor could I blame them.

So after only ten minutes in the bar, I got directions to the Unionville Inn, then I walked outside.

I tried calling Mike Hawthorne's phone. He was still at the hospital, but fortunately he was answering his phone when I called—

"Hey, Marvin. You heard what happened?"

"Yes, I did. Tell me what hospital they're at, and I'll swing by there tomorrow and pay their hospital bills."

"Marvin, that is real fine of you, because those women got a lot of things wrong with them, and Mickey and Jim sure can't pay those bills. I've been trying to get the UMWA national leadership to pay their bills out of emergency funds, but now I don't have to worry about that."

After Mike told me the name of the hospital in Fairmont, and the names of the two women patients, I asked, "So why were Mickey and Jim threatened?"

Mike sighed over the phone. "The exhaust fan for Mine Number 3 was turned off. So there was a buildup of firedamp"—flammable gas—"then everything went to shit."

I remembered the news footage I'd seen, of flames coming up through a fan whose blades were not turning. Aloud, I asked, "Why are Mickey and Jim sure the fan was turned off?"

"It's got a bad bearing, so you can hear it when it's on. But both guys noticed the quiet, just before they went into the rescue chamber. Besides, CI has a history of repairmen here starting a repair job, then CI pulls 'em off-site to fix something at another mine."

I said, "So add in the fact that the sprinkler system was busted and wasn't soaking down the coal dust, and CI is in trouble with the government."

Mike Hawthorne sighed again. "They sure as shit *will* be, if Mickey and Jim tell everything they know. But right now those two are angry, but they're also scared for their wives and kids."

****

I'd been walking toward the Unionville Inn while I was talking to Mike on my smartphone. By the time I ended the call with him, I was almost to the Unionville Inn parking lot.

By now the time was after 11 p.m., and I was feeling exhausted. But while I was still out of earshot of Anna Kay, Almira, and Elvira, I decided to phone my genie.

But when I called Fatima, I heard a message, "The number you have called is not a working number."

Huh? How can this be?

I called Fatima again. This time I was told, "This call cannot be completed as dialed."

This is impossible! Fatima had a magical fake-phone that was directly tied into mine. Not only did this mean that our calls could never be tapped, but it meant that my calls to her, and her calls to me, always went through.

I was trying to figure out how this could be happening, and how to fix it, when I got a horrible thought.

I ran the remaining distance to the Unionville Inn, ran through the parking lot, and jammed my key into the door lock for Room 111.

Nobody was inside.

The television was on; I turned it off. On the dresser by the television were three smartphones, and a plastic ice bucket that had melted ice in it. Both beds were made; though on the twins' bed, two pillows had been pulled out and laid lengthwise against the headboard.

I tried calling Fatima with my smartphone again. I still had no luck connecting with her.

The room phone rang.

Chapter 31
Must I Do This Alone?

When I answered the room phone, I heard, "Marvin, this is Vinnie Lavagetto. You've noticed, you got people missing."

I need to save Anna Kay and the twins! I can't let him kill them!

Calm, I need to stay calm.

I took a deep breath, then said into the phone, "Lavagetto, Fatima told me about you, none of it flattering. I'm not paying a penny in ransom until I know the women are all right."

"Ransom? Do I look like a mook with no imagination?"

"No, you look like a greedy killer. You've built a big empire from blinding and killing your opponents."

"Tell ya what. All three skirts are in the press box of the football stadium for this town's high school. If you can walk out of there with all three women alive and healthy, I'll let you. Won't cost you a fucking dime."

This is way too easy.

I replied, "How generous. But I'm not taking one step till I know they're okay."

"Well, I see a problem with that. Your wife is *busy* right now, and the hottie twins are, shall we say, asleep. So you're gonna have to take my word for it."

What does he mean, she's "busy"?

I said, "Right, take the word of a thug, murderer, extortioner, and now kidnapper."

The women could already be dead.

Lavagetto said, "But what choice do you have? I'll be waiting at the press box when you show up. But don't bring in any donut-chompers, because you know what will happen."

"Yeah. You'll kill all the cops, and smile."

"Don't forget that. By the way, your wife, Anna Whatzerface, has great-looking tits."

If you've raped her, you bastard, I'll—

Lavagetto hung up on me.

****

I need to save them!

But I don't dare go in by myself. I need Fatima.

I tried calling Fatima again on my smartphone. No dice.

I tried calling the kitchen phone at the mansion. I got another "unable to complete this call as dialed" message.

Even worse, right after I hung up—

FOOM.

Kharmesh was the same height as me, and—something I'd never seen before—had the same ultramuscular build as me. But unlike me, Kharmesh had glowing blue eyes, blue skin, and blue Middle Eastern clothing.

Kharmesh gestured toward the smartphone that I was still holding. "I won't let you call Fatima. Forget about it."

"If you think that telling me this will make me quit, you don't know me."

"If you think you can outsmart me, human, *you* don't know *me*." Kharmesh grinned at me, then *foom*ed away.

I tried using my smartphone, then I tried using the room phone. I called Virgilia and everyone else who lived at the mansion and whose phone number I had stored. I spent fifteen minutes doing all that, and got nothing to show for it.

****

I'd given away all my pocket change to Pompadour. I needed more change, for an idea I had.

I discovered that the motel had a little laundry room for customers. By the soap-vendor machine was a change machine. I got two dollars' worth of change.

I walked to the motel office, which was empty when I walked in. In a corner of the room was a pay phone.

I dropped in fifty cents, told the operator I wanted to make a collect call, and gave her the number for the mansion's kitchen phone. I heard the "ringing" tone—

FOOM. From behind, a blue, male hand reached under my arm and pushed down the phone-cradle switch, which killed the call.

As I spun around, I snapped, "Dammit, Kharmesh—"

Except that, while the being was clearly a Blue Tribe *djinni,* he was definitely not Kharmesh. He had ordinary height, and a potbelly.

"Who are *you?*" I said.

He looked me up and down. "Funny, Fatima says she hates Kharmesh, but she made you look just like him. That is, except for your very *human* skin color." He said *human* with all the contempt he could muster.

I said. "I'll ask you again: What's your name?" I shrugged. "I can call you 'Smoky,' it doesn't matter to me."

"You *dare*—"

"Listen, Smoky, you are interfering with my genie-master business, and I bet Solomon's angel would not be happy about such a thing. So please *foom* yourself gone while I make this phone call."

The blue being stood straight. "I am Hakeezib, Chief of the Blue Tribe of Djinn. I will not allow you to telephone Fatima, human."

I said, "You'll pardon me if I don't shake your hand, Hakeezib. But like I told Kharmesh, I'm going to keep trying to contact Fatima."

"No, you will not. Kharmesh's human master is holding your women; and since you care about them, soon you will go to rescue them."

"But without Fatima around. That's your plan."

"Remember, genie-master human, it was *you* who commanded Fatima to not come here."

****

When I walked out of the motel office (and thus, when I walked away from the pay phone), Hakeezib *foom*ed away.

Then as I was walking back to Room 111, a thought came to me. I mentally slapped myself for having been stupid.

Quietly I said, "Fatima, if you're monitoring me with your scrying ball, please find a way to come here without Blue Tribe finding out. If you can't come here without them finding out, find a way to talk to me without them finding out."

I heard no *FOOM*, and I saw nothing different, but I heard Fatima's voice in my ear: "I'm still in the mansion; what you're hearing is an illusionary voice. Master, I ask you to stop walking and to look up at the stars."

I did as requested, and seconds later, I heard in my ear—

"I've created an illusion that your mouth is closed and your face is motionless, except for blinking. Since *I* know it's an illusion, I can penetrate the illusion and read your lips with my scrying ball."

"So you and I can talk without Kharmesh or Hakeezib knowing we're talking?"

"Unless Kharmesh thinks to check for any illusion in your area. I can't promise anything except, He probably won't think to do that."

"Fatima, I need you here. Is there some way you can come here without Blue Tribe knowing?"

"Yes, if I come to Unionville and cast an invisibility illusion on myself. But that will work only till Kharmesh does an illusion-check spell or a locator spell."

"Kharmesh *or Hakeezib*. Only two minutes ago, Hakeezib stopped me from phoning you."

"Yes, I saw." The voice in my ear let loose with sulfuric profanity in a foreign language.

Then Fatima and I worked out how to sneak her into Unionville.

Finally I said, "Before you leave the mansion, there is something I want you to ask SJ-1 and Virgilia to do, and please make a request from me to Ashnadim. These requests are critically important." Then I told Fatima the requests that I wanted her to pass along.

I felt hope then. If Kharmesh and Hakeezib were not excessively cautious, our plan would work.

I recalled back in 2010, when I had first discovered the power of Fatima's illusions. Fatima had created an illusionary 1933 jazz band in the monster kitchen. I had been able to see the instrumentalists and hear them; and I had been able to smell the female vocalist, and flirt with her—but she had not been solid, because she had not been really there.

Fatima's illusions seemed *real*, so I trusted her now to "disappear" when she was actually present.

If Vinnie thought I was coming to rescue the women by myself, but I actually had Fatima with me, this would give me a strong advantage.

On the other hand, if those Blue Tribe *djinn* started to distrust what they were *not* seeing, my life would get difficult.

Fatima's voice in my ear said, "You know that kidnapping Anna Kay and the twins was just a trap to lure you in, right?"

"Yes, a trap," I answered. "And it's working, because I'm going exactly where Lavagetto wants me."

Chapter 32
This Is Way Too Easy

After standing in one spot and staring at the stars, I suddenly looked down and hurried across the Unionville Inn's pavement with a sense of purpose. I went straight to my motel-room door and locked it. I pulled out the rental-truck keys, hurried to where the truck was parked, and was just about to get in the cab and to start the truck, when I paused.

"I might need to put them in the back," I murmured aloud.

I walked to the back of the truck, and raised the rolling door all the way up. I walked around the truck to the driver's door, and only then did I get in the cab and start the truck.

As much as I wanted to drive straight to the high school and then to confront Vinnie (and Kharmesh), I didn't. I drove out of town to Fairmont, to a 24-hour Wal-Mart. In the medical-supplies section of the Wal-Mart pharmacy, I bought an eyepatch.

I had figured it out, and Fatima had confirmed it: For Vinnie to blind me, he first had to look into my "eyes." If he couldn't see one eye, he couldn't blind either eye.

****

Unionville's high school, like everything else of importance in Unionville, was off of Route 250, and so was easy to find.

Once the truck was on the grounds of the high school, and I was slowly driving toward the football stadium in the dark, I became aware of a flashing blue light.

The football field, it turned out, ran east-west, with an oblong running track surrounding the playing field. Beyond the east-side end zone, there was a cinder-block snack shack, which was very locked up at the moment.

Seats for Home fans and Visitors fans were located respectively north and south of the football field and track. At the very top of the Home bleachers was a roofed building, the press box; the wall of the press box that faced the football field was mostly replaced with glass. Through the big windows of the press box, I could see dim red light.

Outside of the running track were tall poles, from which hung halogen lights. All those lights were off now, and so the football field, track, and Visitors bleachers were lit only by starlight and moonlight. A black rectangle, which was blocking stars, was all I could see of the scoreboard.

Most of the Home bleachers were likewise black-dark. One part was lit by—

"Five flashing *blue-neon arrows?* Are you kidding me?" I murmured.

All five blue-neon arrows flashed on and off in unison. They floated in the air, defying gravity. Together, the blue-neon arrows pointed out the walking aisle that went from the bottom of the Home bleachers, all the way up to the side door of the press box.

I parked the truck. As much as I wanted to, I didn't rush out of the cab. I turned on the overhead light, removed the eyepatch from its packaging, and covered my left eye. Then I turned off the overhead light, stepped out of the truck, locked the truck door, and pocketed the rental-truck keys.

To my left, I heard Fatima's voice: "With that eyepatch, you look like a pirate. Or an assassin-spy."

I didn't reply, or turn my head. I just started walking slowly toward the first of the blue arrows.

I "explained" my slow walk by looking around in every direction as I walked, as if I were expecting a pack of dragons to be hiding somewhere in all that blackness.

Of course no dragons actually lurked in the darkness. But neither did I see any gangster sentries anywhere, which flabbergasted me.

When I got to the lowest of the five neon arrows, I reached out and tried to grab it. My hand passed right through the tubing. The arrows were illusion, as I'd suspected.

The walking aisle was narrow; there was no way that invisible Fatima could walk beside me. I didn't know whether she was behind me as I climbed steps, or somehow had gotten ahead of me, or was floating in the air somewhere.

In any case, one minute after I'd passed the first neon arrow, I was at the side door to the press box.

For the first time since Paula Sarin had taken control of Fatima's genie-lamp, I felt fear. *Stark* fear—fear of the unknown, fear of death, and fear of pain.

But Anna Kay, Almira, and Elvira had only one protector against Lavagetto and Kharmesh: me.

I turned the doorknob and opened the press-box door.

Chapter 33
I Unwillingly Shoot Vinnie

I walked into the press box, not shutting the door (so that I didn't accidentally shut the door on invisible Fatima).

The first thing I saw was the twins, *both dead.* The next thing I saw was the gun that had killed them.

Each LeClerc girl was wrapped, from shoulders to toes, in a cocoon of blue neon, and was lying on the floor. They each had been shot in the forehead; blood and brains were splattered on the floor and wall behind them.

Inside the press box were no writing desks as such, but just below the window was a shelf that ran the length of the window, and that was wide enough to support an electric typewriter. On the shelf by the dead twins was a pistol.

At the other end of the room, a blue fireball appeared.

Lit by the blue fireball were three other people: Kharmesh, Anna Kay, and the man whom I recognized from SJ-1's green laptop as Vinnie Lavagetto.

Anna Kay was on her knees in front of Lavagetto, giving him a five-star blowjob. Kharmesh watched me, stonefaced.

I said, "Anna Kay, what the hell are you doing? *Stop that!*" Yes, I was angry; but more than that, I was feeling complete shock.

Anna Kay stopped deepthroating Lavagetto, and turned around to look at me. "Marvin, you're *here?*"

Then Anna Kay's face wrinkled up, and she started crying. "Oh Marvin, I love *you* and I love *him!* I don't know what to do now."

Lavagetto slapped her head. "Get back to sucking my dick, slut. *That's* what you do now."

Anna Kay replied, "But Vinnie sugar, Marvin told me to stop."

Instead of arguing more, Lavagetto grabbed Anna Kay's head and *forced* her to resume sucking him.

I growled in response.

Lavagetto looked at me and taunted, "You don't like me using your wife as a suck-slut? Whaddaya going to *do* about it, huh? You call yourself a *man?*"

What am I going to do, he asks?

I wanted to shove my hand into his chest, yank out his still-beating heart, and stomp it flat.

I wanted to pick him up by his jaw, and smash his head against the wall again and again, till the wall behind his head showed as much blood and brains as behind the twins' heads.

That's what I *wanted* to do. What I *did* do was to grab the gun on the shelf that was within reach.

I was *thisclose* to shooting Lavagetto in the head, when I heard Fatima's voice in my ear—

"The twins are magically asleep, not dead. Their murdered corpses are illusion."

I froze, with the gun pointed at Lavagetto's face but I not pulling the trigger, while Anna Kay sucked Lavagetto's dick (dammit!) and while Kharmesh watched me closely.

They're trying to trick me, so I lose my temper and act on impulse. If I pull this trigger, Kharmesh would be allowed to kill me.

I raised my forearm so that the gun pointed at the ceiling. Aloud, I said, "Lavagetto, I won't try to kill you, no matter how much I want to. And Kharmesh? My Date Of Fated Death isn't for *years* yet; you should have checked first."

Crisis averted, I thought.

****

Lavagetto sent Kharmesh a helpless look: *This isn't in the plan! What do we do now?*

Kharmesh said to him, "Master, I *cannot* kill him if he has not hurt either you or me."

Lavagetto looked at me, and his sneer was almost convincing. "You're not really a man, are you?"

I replied, "Jeez, get a new song. I'm not singing that one."

FOOM. Blue light flashed, then Hakeezib appeared in front of Kharmesh.

Hakeezib said to me, "You acting all noble, human, is stopping Blue Tribe from achieving true glory."

Hakeezib gestured. My elbow straightened, bringing the gun down level. My hand pointed the gun at Lavagetto's forehead, then my finger pulled the trigger. *BANG!*

*****

Of course Lavagetto wasn't killed or even harmed; Kharmesh made sure of that.

Hakeezib gestured again, and my hand tossed the still-smoking gun back onto the wide shelf.

Hakeezib was controlling my hand and arm at the moment, but he wasn't controlling my mouth. Even as I was shooting at Lavagetto and tossing the gun away, I was yelling, "HOUSEKEEPER, FIRE TORPEDOES!"

FOOM. With green flashes, the twins and Anna Kay disappeared from the press box.

Lavagetto and the two Blue Tribe *djinn* had looked confused by my code phrase, before its meaning became clear. Then Hakeezib said, "This is *Fatima's* work! She's not supposed to know yet about—"

Hakeezib summoned his scrying ball. He glanced into it for only an instant before he shot a hand out.

With a flash of blue light, Fatima stood revealed.

Lavagetto said, "Take a last look, bitch. *He's* about to die, and *you're* about to get stuck in your lamp for *years!*"

Fatima's laugh was scornful. "Is *that* what the blue gorilla told you? Then by all means, he needs to get cracking. Even though the only reason Master shot you, *jamoke*, is because Hakeezib made him do it."

I said, "Fatima, please stop."

Then I looked at Kharmesh, trying not to look nervous. Kharmesh couldn't kill me, the universe wouldn't let him, but he could turn me into a paraplegic or quadriplegic.

"DIE, ATTACKER!" Kharmesh thundered. His hands shot out, and a big blue fireball flew across the room—

—which shrank to nothingness as it got near me. I felt a moment's push when hot air hit my chest, that's all.

"WHAT THE FUCK?" Lavagetto yelled.

I replied, "My Date Of Fated Death isn't for at least six years yet. You can't kill me today."

"Oh, *yeah?*" Lavagetto said. He walked up close to me, grabbed the gun off the shelf (which I let him do), and pointed the gun at me. He said to me, "You die now."

Fatima said, "If you even *scratch* Master, human, I get to ruin your day."

"Enough talk," Lavagetto said.

CLICK. Then CLICK, CLICK, CLICK!

I said, "Too bad, your gun's jammed. And so long as you keep trying to kill me, it'll *stay* jammed."

He smiled cruelly at me. "*Be blind!*"

"Peekaboo, I see you," I replied.

"This is fucked up," Lavagetto said, shoving the gun in its holster and walking away.

I looked at Kharmesh and Hakeezib, and *smiled*. "Fatima has moved the women to someplace where you won't find them, and I'm still alive. Come, Fatima, we're leaving."

"Not so fast, human," Hakeezib said.

****

Hakeezib said to me, "I want you and Green Tribe Bitch to see something amazing."

Foom. After the blue flash, I saw—

"A dead puppy, yucch." The puppy's eyes were cloudy, it had fly eggs filling its nostrils, rigor mortis had set in, and the corpse was starting to stink.

Hakeezib gave Fatima a meaningful look. "Seventeen hours ago, this dog's Date Of Fated Death was over fourteen solar years from now."

Fatima looked horrified. "That's impossible! Only God or a bound *djinni* granting a wish can change a creature's Date Of Fated Death."

Hakeezib smiled at me. "Actually, all it takes is thirty Blue Tribe *djinn* working together. But we didn't know that before now, because Blue Tribe didn't care when a human died."

Hakeezib gestured, my ears popped, then I was outside.

****

Around me, lights came on, but blue lights instead of white. I saw that I stood on the 50-yard line of the high-school football field. In bright blue light, I saw the goalposts, the snack shack, my rental truck near the snack shack, and the chain-link fence that separated the football field from the track. A team bench was set at both the north and south ends of the 50-yard line.

FOOM. An instant after I was *foom*ed to the football field, Fatima appeared next to me.

Hakeezib waved both hands, and a whole bunch of blue message-lightballs shot out from his hands. They flew away going north, south, east, and west; and even flew straight into the ground at an angle.

Meanwhile, Lavagetto was running down the steps from the press box, with Kharmesh providing a blue fireball to see by. Lavagetto demanded, "Kharmesh, what's going on? Why did your boss take Harper onto the football field?"

Hakeezib said, "Be quiet, human. You *failed* to get Fatima's master to shoot you, so I have no use for you."

FOO-F-FOO-FOO-FOOM. Blue Tribe *djinn* appeared on the football field. At the same time—

Hakeezib's hands flashed blue; and something like a blue, glowing airbag slammed into Fatima. Her body was pushed up and she flew all the way downfield and beyond; she punched through the end-zone fence, and slammed against the cinder-block rear wall of the snack shack. *WHACK!*

"FATIMA!" I yelled. I started to run to her—

But then I couldn't, because suddenly I was bound in a blue-neon cocoon.

I could only wait helplessly to see what had happened to Fatima.

For several seconds, she lay in a crumpled heap on the ground. Then she stood up, and shook her head to clear it.

FOO-FOOM. I couldn't see Fatima anymore after that, because now there were Blue Tribe *djinn* forming a ring around me; beyond them, a line of blue *djinn* faced Fatima.

From where Fatima had to be, suddenly I saw a burst of green message-lightballs fly in every direction.

Hakeezib smiled. "So now it begins. When Green Tribe and Pink Tribe arrive, we will finally fight the Djinn War."

"Blue Tribe will lose," I said. "And I'll see it all."

"Human, you won't see anything. You are about to die."

Chapter 34
My Date Of Fated Death: Today

Hakeezib spoke foreign words, and all the *djinn* in the ring turned to face me. Many were grinning in anticipation.

Hakeezib had brought spares. He'd told me that he needed thirty Blue Tribe *djinn* for his spell to work; but a quick estimate told me that there were many more than thirty *djinn* making up the ring.

Now Hakeezib spoke more foreign words, and the *djinn* in the ring each turned a quarter turn to the right.

Hakeezib commanded again, and the ring *djinn* start to walk in a counterclockwise direction. As they walked around me, they chanted words in unison—

Jonva paiza myusa garma. Faupo trenko kyario byonkso.

—and they pointed to me with their left hands in unison.

Hakeezib asked me mockingly, "How are you feeling, human? Any pain? Discomfort?"

"I'm feeling fine," I replied. "Your 'killer' spell isn't working."

"It is," he replied. "But you're healthy for a human, so you won't feel it at first."

Hakeezib gestured. I rose up off the ground a few feet, rotated half a turn, then dropped to the ground. Now I could see the scoreboard.

Floating in front of the scoreboard was a giant glowing-blue hourglass. A small cone of glowing-blue sands were already on the bottom. But now sands weren't *falling* through the tiny opening, they were *spurting* through.

Next to the hourglass was a column of seven floating spheres. Each sphere was barely glowing a dull blue.

Hakeezib said, "Seven times, anti-clockwise, will the magic dancers orbit you. When they have danced seven orbits, today will be your Date Of Fated Death. When that happens, human, you will be slaughtered like a pig."

I smiled at him. "But before I die, Smoky, I'll see Blue Tribe losing the Djinn War."

****

A chain-link gate allowed entry through the fence that surrounded the football field. Vinnie stood at the gate with Kharmesh, watching things happen on the football field.

Vinnie didn't understand half of what he was seeing. Except that when Green-Eyed Bitch got knocked all the way into the cinder-block building—that sure had to hurt.

Good. The bitch deserves it.

Vinnie asked, "What they're doing, it'll kill the goody-two-shoes, and the bitch will have to go back into her lamp?"

Kharmesh said, "Yes, Master, this is Blue Tribe's plan."

"What's to stop the bitch from hocus-pocusing Harper out of here, like she did with the skirts?"

"To do that, she has to see him. But where she's at, she can't see him."

"But you guys can pop up anywhere, right? So she could pop inside the circle and then disappear him."

"Hakeezib is standing next to Harper, to knock Fatima on her ass if she tries that shit."

"That's not enough. I want *you* there too, next to Harper. Stop anyone from interfering with his getting killed."

"You're *ordering* me to fight Fatima and Green Tribe? Not a problem, Master."

FOOM. Kharmesh was gone.

****

FOOM. In a flash of blue light, Kharmesh appeared next to me.

Great, just what I needed. Because I was starting to feel dizzy.

Kharmesh grinned at me. "I hope to see Fatima's face when she gets yanked back into her lamp. Which will happen the instant you die."

I made no reply.

FOOM. Fatima appeared in front of me. "Master, we—"

FLUP. Kharmesh hit Fatima with an repulsion-spell, and Fatima went flying over the ring-dancers' heads.

FOOM. FLUP. Now it was Kharmesh who went flying away; two ring-dancers had to duck. Behind me, a voice said, "Pink Tribe stands with Green Tribe, Hakeezib."

Hakeezib replied, "Pink Tribe *djinn* are silly fools, Sigvard." Then Hakeezib's hands flashed blue. FLUP.

FOO-FOOM. FLUP. Now it was Hakeezib knocked out of the ring.

I didn't look to see who in Green Tribe or Pink Tribe had cast the latest repulsion-spell. The topmost of the seven orbit-count spheres now was glowing bright blue.

I felt an ache in my left arm.

FOOM. Fatima appeared in front of me, but her clothes were dirty. Fatima said, "Master—"

FOO-FOOM. Whoever they were, they appeared behind me.

Fatima ran toward me. "—we—"

FLUP.

Fatima was knocked away before she could finish the sentence.

****

The ring-dancers had completed three orbits. Now the bottom of the hourglass had more sand than at the top.

I had a chest pain that came and went. Kharmesh (when Green Tribe or Pink Tribe wasn't sending him flying) now had a blurry face, because I was getting farsighted. One of my teeth hurt.

I felt bedraggled, and Fatima looked bedraggled. Her clothing was dirty, her arms and face were dirty, and her formerly flawless black hair (the envy of every woman at the mansion) now had split ends and was frizzy. Fatima moved slower now.

Fatima had not yet managed to *foom* me away from the middle of the ring, though she kept trying.

FOOM. Fatima appeared inside the ring of Blue Tribe dancers yet again. FLUP. And got knocked flying yet again—

—an instant before the Blue Tribe *djinn* who had repulsed Fatima, were themselves repulsed by *djinn* from Green Tribe and Pink Tribe.

Green Tribe and Pink Tribe had tried repulsing the ring-dancers. But even when some ring-dancers were missing from the ring, the remaining ring-dancers moved to evenly space themselves in the ring, and kept chanting and dancing.

In any case, even with fewer ring-dancers in the ring, the rushing of sands in the hourglass did not slow down at all.

By no means were all the repulsion-spells being cast inside the ring. Beyond the ring and everywhere in the football stadium, there was a continuous spectacle of blue-, green-, and pink-clad bodies being knocked into the air.

I said to Hakeezib, who was standing to my left at the time, "There sure are a lot of Blue Tribe *djinn* getting knocked around. You're right to worry now."

Hakeezib glared. "Be quiet, human. Show respect."

I laughed. "Or else what, you'll kill me?"

"Blue Tribe is *not* losing."

"Yeah, sure, and I'm King Solomon in disguise."

By now, the football stadium was messed up. Apparently a *djinni* could harden his body at will; so the stadium looked like someone had been firing 100-, 200-, or 300-pound cannonballs around. Two of the tall metal lightpoles were knocked down, the press box was caved in, and there were big holes punched through the stadium seats. I heard a steady chorus of BANGs and CLANGs.

****

Now six of the seven orbit-count spheres were bright blue. The hourglass showed hardly any sand at the top.

My back hurt, my kidneys hurt, my teeth hurt, my heart hurt, and now even the ring-dancers were blurry to my one uncovered eye.

I figured I had only minutes left to live.

Especially since Vinnie Lavagetto was standing just beyond the ring-dancers, he was smiling coldly at me, and he had his gun in his hand.

FOOM. Fatima was inside the ring again.

She moved slowly now, and her waist-length ponytail now had more short, broken-off black hairs outside the green cincher than were contained by the cincher. She didn't use her left arm any more than she had to. She was filthy.

And yet she kept trying to rescue me, even though Blue Tribe thwarted her every time.

I looked her in the eyes. I said with feeling, "I love—"

FLUP. Fatima got repulsed out of earshot.

Fifteen seconds passed before she *foom*ed back inside the dancer-ring again.

"—you."

Goodbye, Mom. Goodbye, Dad. Goodbye, Anna Kay. I treasure the love and happiness you've all given me.

I couldn't say *I love you* to anyone else, but at least I'd squared the ledger with Fatima.

I looked up at the stars—the only things I could see clearly without glasses. I prayed, for the first time since middle school: "God, when I die, whatever happens next, happens. But I ask you to bless Anna Kay and Fatima, and even Almira and Elvira. They all caught lots of shit tonight because of me, so please be nice to them. Amen."

But while I talked nice to God, talking to Hakeezib was another story. I looked over at Hakeezib and said, "Ha, like I've been saying: Blue Tribe is losing."

Then everything happened at once.

****

Inside the ring, Kharmesh's chin came up, and his spine straightened, as if he'd been goosed in the ass. Then—

"My master summons me," Kharmesh said. *FOOM.*

FOOM. A Green Tribe *djinni* appeared inside the ring. I didn't know his name, but he, Ashnadim, and I had pushed the hallway rug up my staircase in 2010.

The Green Tribe *djinni*'s hands came up, to repulse Hakeezib out of the ring. But Hakeezib was faster.

But this time, Hakeezib didn't *repulse* the Green Tribe *djinni*, Hakeezib—

FOOM.

—*water-swapped* him. Suddenly a column of briny water was collapsing where the Green Tribe *djinni* had stood. Hakeezib said, "Blue Tribe will *not* lose this war!"

All the *djinn* combatants inside the ring, except for Hakeezib, froze in shock. Blue, Green, or Pink, they all stopped and stared.

The ring-dancers stopped moving, except to turn their heads and stare at the place where the slain *djinni* had stood.

Overhead, floating *djinn* had been throwing fireballs at each other, but now they likewise froze. Then a Green Tribe *djinni* yelled, "Blue Tribe has water-swapped Nadaar!"

From every green-dressed and pink-dressed *djinni* came a scream of rage.

****

"ENOUGH!" a voice yelled from overhead. "MAKE END TO YOUR BATTLES!"

I looked up (as did every other being, including the *djinn* floating in the air). Up in the air, and descending slowly, was a white-winged, white-robed, silver-eyed angel.

"PERSIST NOT IN THIS ABOMINATION!" the angel then said. "BEGONE!" There were simultaneous flashes of white light, then every one of the ring-dancers was gone.

I looked up at the blue hourglass. Only a few glowing-blue sands remained at the top; but now, no sands were falling.

FOOM. Kharmesh and three other beings appeared inside the ring of dancers then—or rather, inside where the ring had just been.

"One wish made, one wish granted," Kharmesh said.

With Kharmesh were SJ-1, who was holding her green GT Technologies laptop; Virgilia, who was holding a brass oil lamp that was shinier than mine; and Bashira, a Green Tribe *djinni* who, Virgilia assured me, "liked humans."

SJ-1 didn't hang around to chat; she immediately ran off toward limping Fatima.

Meanwhile, Lavagetto was yelling, "NO-O-O!" Before I could even yell, he had aimed his gun and fired at Virgilia. "That's *mine!*" he yelled. "You stole it!"

A breeze mussed Virgilia's hair for a second, but otherwise she was fine.

Kharmesh said to Lavagetto, "No honor. You're *stupid*, too." Kharmesh grinned a shark's smile at Lavagetto.

The angel said: "HOLD, BOUND DJINNI KHARMESH. VENGEANCE IS MINE, SAITH THE LORD; I WILL REPAY."

Lavagetto suddenly was immobilized with manacles, fetters, and *lots* of chains, all of which were glowing white.

Hakeezib was likewise instantly white-shackled.

Seeing all this, every being was stunned motionless and silent. Every being, that is, except for Fatima, who was limping toward me with SJ-1's help; and Virgilia, who asked Kharmesh, "What are those blue-neon things that are wrapped around Marvin?"

Kharmesh replied, "Those are magical restraints, Master."

Virgilia said, "For my second wish, I wish that Marvin Harper be free of all restraints, whether magical or physical."

Seconds later, Kharmesh had not even finished saying *One wish made, one wish granted* when—

—Virgilia thrust Kharmesh's lamp into my hands. "Take it," she said.

I did. Even though I was feeling like shit, I managed to rub the lamp.

FOOM. Blue light flashed, then Kharmesh was standing directly in front of me. He said, "Greetings, Master of the—"

I managed to raise my hand. "Later."

"Oh fuck, fuck, *fuck*," shackled Lavagetto said.

The angel turned to look at me. "BE WHOLE, MARVIN STEVEN HARPER. EVERYTHING THAT WAS TAKEN FROM YOU TONIGHT, IS RESTORED."

Suddenly I felt young again, and strong, and virile. The blue hourglass now looked the same as when the ring-dancers had started, with most of its sands at the top.

Even the rental truck, which had caught fire at some point in the battle, now looked the same as when I'd parked it.

****

Then the angel rebuked Lavagetto—

You have killed many strangers, even children. You would have killed Marvin Harper too, to fulfill your ambition that is contrary to the intent of Solomon's rule. You magicked Ruslana Dubova, Jenny Lawrence, and Anna Kay Harper into breaking their marriage vows.

The angel rebuked Hakeezib—

You schemed to use Marvin Harper as your way to cause the war of <u>djinn</u>. When Marvin Harper, by cooling his anger, thwarted your scheme, you forced him to attempt murder as your scheme required. You used harmful magic on Marvin Harper as your bait to compel the bound <u>djinni</u> Fatima, the green tribe of <u>djinn</u>, and the pink tribe of <u>djinn</u> to do battle against you.

Then the angel said, "TO WHOM MUCH IS GIVEN, MUCH IS REQUIRED. BEHOLD THE WRATH OF GOD."

Hakeezib lifted up his head and screamed. Then his scream was cut off, as his skin and clothing turned white; Hakeezib was being covered with frost. It took only seconds for Hakeezib to freeze solid.

When I looked over at Lavagetto, I was confused at first: How had his father replaced him in the shackles? Then I realized that twenty-six-year-old Lavagetto was aging rapidly. As I watched, he aged right out of his forties into his fifties.

Less than a minute later, he had died of old age. Even then, his body continued to age rapidly: It took less than a minute for his corpse to become a skeleton.

The angel, who had been floating in the air all this time, came down to earth by the two punished beings. The angel picked up one of Lavagetto's upper-leg bones and, swinging it like a sledgehammer, struck it hard against frozen-Hakeezib. Frozen-Hakeezib shattered into gravel-sized pieces.

No *djinni* objected.

Chapter 35
Elvira Surprises Me

After healing me, the angel praised Fatima, then healed her as well.

The angel didn't repair any of the damage to property, except for my rental truck. By now, the football stadium was completely trashed—

Only two lightpoles *weren't* knocked down or bent, both the Home and Visitors seats had man-sized holes punched in them, the chain-link fence was down everywhere, and one of the goalposts was flattened. The scoreboard was tilted. Both team benches were laying on the track. The cinder-block snack shack had cracks in the wall that faced the field.

The angel, and Lavagetto's skeleton, both flashed white and disappeared. Immediately after, I heard *FOOM*s and saw different-colored flashes, as individual *djinn* disappeared.

I gave Kharmesh thirty minutes to say goodbye to his Blue Tribe friends and relatives, before he was to go back into the lamp. Kharmesh looked shocked at this order, but I thought that sending him straight into the lamp was cruel.

Fatima frowned at my generosity with Kharmesh, but didn't say anything.

I profusely thanked Green Tribe *djinni* Bashira, even though I'd just met her, for helping Virgilia and SJ-1 with their search for where Lavagetto kept his things.

(Kharmesh's lamp, it turned out, had been in a storage locker that Vinnie Lavagetto had rented. Lavagetto had rented the storage locker in the name of "Vinnie Vega," who was a *Pulp Fiction* character who was a hit man. *Lazy.*)

By the time Kharmesh was blue-smoked into the lamp, I'd long since removed the eyepatch and had tossed it into a trash can by the snack shack. I did not need the eyepatch anymore, and I did *not* want it as a souvenir!

****

By the time I unlocked the door to the rental truck—
• Lavagetto's skeleton and the angel had both vanished in a flash of white light,
• all three Tribes' *djinn* had *foom*ed away,
• Kharmesh was back in his lamp, and
• frozen-Hakeezib's graveled body had sublimated into blue smoke and had drifted away.

So by then, Fatima and I were the only beings in the football stadium.

For some reason that I've never figured out, Reader, even though the Djinn War was making noise and was causing fires at the football stadium, no police and no firemen ever came out to investigate. (For which I'm glad, actually; the responders would have all been killed.) So when Fatima and I (and Kharmesh's lamp) got in the rental truck and I drove away, no human took note of us.

Minutes later, the truck was idling behind the Unionville McDonald's, which was empty and dark. I put Kharmesh's lamp inside a cardboard box marked "French Fries," and threw that cardboard box in the Dumpster. It was only later, Reader, that I realized that I'd disposed of a genie lamp without making even one wish with its genie.

I remarked to Fatima, "Aladdin's lamp, now in the trash can. How ironic."

Fatima replied, "Kharmesh in the garbage, how deserved."

Minutes after I got rid of Kharmesh's lamp, the truck was parked at the Unionville Inn, as Fatima and I entered the motel room.

From the motel room, Fatima *foom*ed us to my old bedroom in my parents' house. This was where Anna Kay and the twins were magically sleeping.

****

At my request, Fatima timed the "awaken" spell so that Anna Kay awoke when I kissed her. However, I should mention that Disney's Snow White has a much flatter chest than Anna Kay has.

Anna Kay sat up and looked around my old bedroom. "Marvin? Such a weird dream I had, and it seemed so *real!*"

"Oh? Tell me your dream."

"We and the twins flew to West Virginia, and then the twins and me got kidnapped and taken to a football stadium, and then I met the guy who'd ordered us kidnapped, then I—oh god!" Anna Kay covered her face with her hands.

I said very gently, "Anna Kay, that wasn't a dream, it was real. It was *magic*." I gestured to the other side of the room, where the still-sleeping twins lay on the floor, each still wrapped in a blue-neon cocoon.

Anna Kay gasped when she saw the twins.

"No, *no*," she said, fiercely shaking her head. "It can't be real, because then when you walked in, I was. . ." She couldn't finish the sentence.

I said, "It was real, and you really did that. But it's okay, because you weren't in control."

The bedroom door opened then. Standing there was my father, wearing a bathrobe; my mother, in a bathrobe, stood behind him.

Dad said, "Hi, Anna Kay, glad to see you're awake. Hi, Fatima."

Dad looked at me with a raised eyebrow.

I took a deep breath and said, "Anna Kay, there's something that I should have told you before now. It's about Fatima and me."

Anna Kay smirked. "What, that you two have some sexual position you like, that nobody else has heard of?"

Dad said, "You're right, Marvin, you should have told her before now."

Mom said, "I'll put coffee on."

****

Anna Kay didn't *really* believe what my parents, Fatima, and I had told her. Not until Fatima *foom*ed all three of us, plus cocooned Almira and Elvira, from my old bedroom to the motel room in Unionville.

But by the time that Anna Kay had watched Fatima vanish the twins' blue-neon cocoons, and then awaken both twins from across the room, Anna Kay was a true believer.

The twins spent their first five minutes awake in asking me questions. But no matter what *What* question they asked, or what *How* question they asked, my answer was always the same: "It was magic."

After several minutes, Elvira started giving Fatima a long, studying look.

****

Soon after this, I nodded at Fatima. She then told the four of us goodbye, walked out of the motel room—and the next time any of us saw her again, it was at the mansion.

****

Hours later, I had taken off from Fairmont, and had just reached cruising altitude, when the cockpit door opened.

Elvira said, "Hey, Anna Kay, you mind if I talk to Marvin alone?"

Anna Kay gave me a *Do you know what this is about?* look; I shrugged. Anna Kay smiled at Elvira, said "Be my guest," and walked out of the cockpit.

Elvira slipped into the copilot's seat, then said, "I've talked it over with Almie. When we get home, we're going to Rhonda's house and tell her we're really sorry."

Recall, Reader, that Rhonda was the hostess whose party the twins had crashed in 2010; and when Rhonda had ordered the party-crashers to leave, the twins had threatened to plant drugs in Rhonda's toilet and then to call the sheriff.

Now I replied, "It's good that Almira suggested the apology. And Elvira, I'm very pleased that you agreed to it."

Elvira said, "Then you'll like this even better: It wasn't Almie's idea, it was mine."

Elvira had surprised me many times since I'd met her at the costume party; this was a rare time when the surprise was a good one. I asked her, "Why did *you* decide to tell Rhonda you're sorry?"

She said, "That night, do you know how many women came with us to Rhonda's party?"

"There were six of you," I replied. "You all walked past me when you first arrived."

"That's right, four 'friends' came with us to that party. You want to know how many of them visited Almie or me in prison, even one time? *None.*"

"Where are you going with this?"

"Yesterday after you left the motel room, and before we all got kidnapped, I went to the ice machine to get ice. *Two different people* stopped to tell me that you were a great man for coming there and helping out, and they *thanked me* for coming with you. I didn't tell them that I didn't want to come. You're a hero, and they treated *me* like a hero!"

"Which is lots nicer than nobody coming to visit you."

"Damned stra—I mean, yes."

Elvira's eyes bored into mine. "You're *amazingly* tall, *amazingly* strong, and *amazingly* rich. Fatima calls you 'Master' *all the time*. Last night, when Anna Kay and Almie and I got taken to the football stadium, *weird* shit happened. Which you say was magic."

She's wise to me. I paused, then said, "Go on."

"Marvin, I won't ever ask you how you got the life you have. Though I suspect I know. Anyway, now you're on top. Every day, you could act like the biggest dickhead on the planet, because nobody could stop you. If I were in your shoes, I'd act like a Class-One jerk."

"You would?"

"Total asshole. But instead, you *help* people."

Elvira's right hand pushed an imaginary something away. "No more Miss Bitch for me. From now on, I'm going to be good. Like *you're* good."

THE END